PRECIOUS
BLOOD

BILL O'SULLIVAN

PRECIOUS BLOOD

SOHO

Published by
Soho Press Inc.
853 Broadway
New York, NY 10003

Library of Congress Cataloging-in-Publication Data

O'Sullivan, Bill, 1944–
Precious blood / Bill O'Sullivan.
p.   cm.
ISBN 0-939149-67-2:
I. Title.
PS3565.S89P7   1992
813′.54—dc20   91-47500
CIP

Manufactured in the United States

10   9   8   7   6   5   4   3   2   1

Book design and composition by
The Sarabande Press

To Diana

PRECIOUS BLOOD

THIS IS THE story of Mike Driscoll and how he killed his father.

Like all stories it has many beginnings. Let's start with that cold spring morning in Brooklyn not long after World War II when Mike's father, Jimmy, was retelling the tale of how he and his brother, Fínín, stole the lid from Dónal Mór's coffin back home in Erin across the waves.

This was a tale that always disturbed Mike and he would have preferred listening to the story about the locomotive leaving the tracks, or the Volunteers trying to blow up the Peelers' barracks, or the King of Ireland's son in the Eastern World or the hunchback that the *síoganna* removed the hump from and the other hunchback who ended up with two of them because he wanted something for nothing.

In the morning Mike had his father all to himself and didn't have to share him with his older brother and sister, Eamonn and Peggy. Mike felt they were always hogging life, leaving him last on line. It seemed most everything he had was a hand-me-down, clothes and toys from his brother; even the bed he slept

3

in had been his sister's originally. This morning time with his father, though, was his and no one else's.

He sat at the kitchen table and listened to his father talk. The window behind them was open a bit at the bottom and the curtain billowed out in the cold breeze. Dry leaves could be heard cartwheeling on the rough cement in the alleys as the early sun grabbed at the edges of buildings. Curious fingers of light poked into backyards while small birds sang their hearts out on the empty clotheslines that stretched between the red brick tenements.

Jimmy had made tea as usual, fogging the window as the kettle boiled and whistled. He was eating a soft-boiled egg and he gave Mike the top off it as he always had done since Mike was very small. A circle of white, a smaller circle of yolk, a dot of butter with a dash of pepper floating in it. Mike ate his bit of egg and chewed on a slice of rye bread. Its tartness made his mouth water. Rye was his favorite bread although he would eat only the packaged kind from Catalano's grocery store. He didn't like the bakery sort with the tough crust and the caraway seeds that his mother loved. The caraways reminded him of baby cockroaches. The rye from Catalano's had a soft crust with little round bumps on the bottom of it, the same design as was on the glass bricks that decorated the sidewalk in front of Kleinberg's Laundry.

"It was me brother Fínín and meself," his father began. "We were *garsúns* and we thought it would be a wonderful thing entirely to have a boat of our own and be floating around on the *góilín* like two young gentlemen. The *góilín* was the place the river met the bay. Of course we didn't have a boat and none was to be begged or borrowed, as people got their living from boats back home and there wasn't any pleasure craft as you've here. So we were looking for a substitute."

"So you took a coffin," volunteered Mike.

"Don't be getting ahead of me, *a mhic-ó*," replied Jimmy. "Sure it wasn't the coffin itself but the lid of it. The part they screw down on you when they've got you in it. They've genuine coffins at home, y'know. No puttin' time out with fancy hinges and high polish. *Dhera*, who's go'n to be appreciating fine work when you're under the narrow cloak of the clay as *mo mhóirín*, me grandmother, used be saying. Well and good.

"Now a man was dead by the name of Dónal Mór and his people was waiting on the coffin to bring his body to the chapel. The last night they take the bodies to the chapel and place them up right in front of the altar, at home."

"Why's that?" Mike asked.

"The clergy don't want the people having sport with death. In the ould days it was different. They used be having grand wakes, dancing and matchmaking and the likes, and the clergy put a stop to them." His father spoke disapprovingly.

"Mammy says we should respect priests because they have secret powers," said Mike.

"Secret powers?" said Jimmy. "*Dhera*, they can turn bread and wine into silver."

"You better not let Mammy hear you say that," said Mike.

"Och, your mother's superstitious. God bless her and a finer woman never walked the earth," replied Jimmy. "She believes in all the *piseoga*, all the nonsense, they've got at home. It's because her people gets warnings, y'know, of death approaching. Signs and such. That's the way it is at home with them. Far downs, they are. *Olltachs,* y'know."

"Do the Driscolls get warnings too?" Mike asked.

"Not in my time they didn't, but the ould people told me there was a man of my tribe on a boat once that heard a cow lowing for her calf two days from land. And then the boat went over on its side and the crew looked and what did they see but a man holding on to the chain-plates, and the mate of the ship he told the Driscoll man to hit the bugger for he was going to sink them and bring them down to the bottom. Well, there was such confusion on the mind of the Driscoll man that he didn't know what in all Erin he would do, so it was the mate himself who hit the blackguard, three times on the crown of his head it was with a handspike, till the man of the sea let go his grip and then the boat righted itself. Well, to make it short, the Driscoll man on his next voyage was going over to *Sasana* and the boat foundered off Land's End and every person of the crew was drowned, every mother's son of them including Driscoll himself. Och, but didn't his corpse turn up on the tide at home two days later? The ould ones said it was the man of the sea sailed him home to his people."

"Jeez!" sighed Mike with wide eyes.

"*Ara,* I'll believe it when I see it, *Micilín.* Every ould person at home had seven times seven stories that would put you from sleep for a month. Och, God above us, what *piseoga!* The ould ones had them. They would keep the water they washed the corpse with under the bed until the wake was complete and the body in the ground. They said there was a cure in it. They used put it in little bottles like it was holy water, like the Lourdes

Water ye get here. Och, but they stopped that when I was a *garsún* as nobody could remember what the cure was for anymore!"

Jimmy began roaring with laughter.

"Couldn't remember what it was for!" he repeated and laughed till tears came to his eyes.

Mike couldn't bring himself to share his father's laughter. He was thinking about having such water sprinkled on him and it made his flesh crawl.

"My story," Jimmy said after collecting himself. "Dónal Mór and his funeral. Well, me brother Fínín and meself saw the lid of the coffin out behind me father's shop. Leaning against the wall it was and we thought to ourselves that surely we could make better use of it on a fine warm day than Dónal Mór according as he was dead. So we grabbed the lid and off with the two of us down the *bóithrín*, the lane to the river. And didn't we have it out on the water quicker than you could turn your fist? And didn't we spend the day floating on the *góilín* where the salt water meets the fresh?"

"What did your father do?" Mike asked.

"He had to make another lid, of course." Jimmy replied jokingly. "And when he saw us that evening coming in he came after us with the adze he had in his hand for he had a fiery temper. But we escaped and he soon forgot about it. We kept that coffin lid all summer and great sport we had with it. The evenings were the grandest. Ye don't get evenings like that over here. Sure the sun never sets at home till almost midnight at St. John's Eve in mid-summer. It was like being a prince. The water was so calm sometimes that you'd think you could pole your way south to Spain without stop nor stay as if it were just over the horizon.

"Ah, there was many a man from our parts that joined the Spanish fleet in the ould days, fighting the *Sasanachs* they were. In the ould times, every Gael was automatically a citizen of Spain if he went there, with all the rights and privileges. I would dream when I was your age about Spain, sailing to Cadiz and the Groyne and Seville where the Christmas oranges came from. I would dream about the Spanish Main and South America, about Peru and Panama about Buenos Aires, Valparaiso, Santiago.

"Did you know it was a fella the name of MacKenna laid out that town? Oh, the Gaels could do great things down there, hold their heads high, not like at home in Erin. Santiago, Buenos Aires, Valparaiso. Aren't they fine names now? Did ye know that the water runs down the drain the opposite way down in South America? Did you know that? It runs counterclockwise here and clockwise there. Isn't that something? Couldn't ye see me down there in Valparaiso, *a mhic*, sitting in a warm tub all day watching the water go down the drain?"

Jimmy had a faraway look in his eye as if he were staring down one of those long tree-shaded boulevards this MacKenna had built. He may have been dreaming of the Garden of Mérida, whose story he'd often told Mike, where time stopped for an hour each night so you could grab the magic apple that cured the world's ills while its fierce guardian beasts were stilled, as if frozen under druid spell, and the air was filled only with the memory of sweet birdsong. Maybe he was dreaming of the Princess of the Eastern World who'd married a king of Ireland's son and her yellow hair flooding his shoulders. Maybe he was a bit sad that he'd never get to Spain or Valparaiso but if he was, he was still filled with a kind of happy expectation that there was something bright, burning over the horizon of tomorrow. He'd often told Mike that in the old times, even before Ciarán had brought them the Faith, that the Driscolls had sailed the great ocean, testing the edge of the western seas while the other tribes were fighting each other over the kingship of Caiseal. It was them who'd sighted the Azores and Hy Brasil from which the country of Brazil got its name and they'd gone ashore in America long before Breandán, that Kerryman who got the credit for it.

But for Mike, Jimmy's faraway look was not one of discovery or hope. For him it were as if Jimmy were looking at him from a great distance, as if his father was slipping away over the water on that coffin lid into the realm of death. It was as if Jimmy Driscoll had somehow sealed his fate with this one boyhood prank years before and that there was nothing now but the transparent barrier of time between him and extinction. There is no doubt that Mike had somehow picked up this fatal notion from his mother, Annie O'Shiel, even though she had never spoken to him about the Handsome Man.

ANOTHER BEGINNING. TWENTY-FIVE years earlier. Hot night and the old man was drunk again. He'd be starting up soon. She wished she could escape before he began. She wished she could go to Coney Island to escape him and the heat. To escape. She could almost smell the cotton candy and the salt-water taffy, the boiling ears of yellow corn and the French-fried potatoes bubbling up in the oil. She could almost smell that salt-air smell rolling in from the beach and hear the laughter and the squeals as the roller coaster shot down the first hill. She could almost hear and smell it all on the heavy, sticky air that was coming in the window where her mother sat, head bowed, sewing. Her brother had rushed the growler for the old man from the speakeasy round the corner a half an hour before, sipping at the beer on his way up the stairs. She'd seen him wiping the foam off his lips with the back of his hand on the landing before he'd come in the apartment. The hall door was open because of the heat. He'd turn out just like the old man if he didn't watch his step. The old man was at the kitchen table and the growler was half-empty already. He was mumbling nastily to himself, his eyes squinting at the wet rings on the wood where the growler and his glass had sweated. Flies walked gingerly around the circles, drawn by the odor of the hops. He swept them away with the back of his hand and tipped over his beer glass in the process.

"Fuckin' bastards!" he screamed. "Fuckin' bastards!"

The flies scattered, buzzing around the room before landing once again on the table. They looked like they were washing their front feet in the puddle of spilt beer. The old man took a long slug of whiskey out of the jelly jar. He slammed his fist down on the table.

He was starting up for sure. She knew his routine. As terrible as it was, it was still a routine. First came the cursing and mumbling, then he'd punch out at whoever was nearest to him, or at whoever he'd taken a dislike to at the moment.

Her mother wasn't even looking. She kept her eyes down on her work. She was sweating all over and the girl could see the outline of her breasts and nipples through the cotton smock that clung to her skin. The girl looked at her own body. Her breasts were almost as large and full as her mother's and though she was only fifteen men were already whispering things to her when she passed them on the street. Her mother was always telling her to be careful of men.

"You look like a woman but you're still only a girl," she'd say.

She'd have given anything to have been a woman at that moment. Dressed up in high heels with rouge on her lips she'd have promenaded down the boardwalk all the way to Brighton Beach with the surf whooshing and the men whispering things to her about her body while the salt air rushed its light fingers through her hair.

There was a large drop of sweat beading up on the tip of her mother's nose. Her mother sniffed and shook her head quickly, trying to shake it off. She was working with her hands and couldn't afford to wipe it away. She was doing piece work where speed was everything. The girl walked over and wiped the sweat away with the tail of her dress.

"Don't be showin' off what you got, you little whore," snapped the old man, looking at her exposed thigh.

Quickly the girl let the tail of her dress drop. She said nothing in reply. The old man cursed to himself and shifted in his chair uncomfortably, impatiently. She wondered what he was so angry at, staring at the beer rings and the parish calendar on the wall with the blue fishes marking Fridays. The old man emptied his pockets on the table and began counting his money. The coins and bills were wet with beer. She watched as he took another sip out of the jelly jar full of whiskey. The old man was worse when he drank booze. It was Mr. Begley on the third floor who'd given it to him. He made it in his bathtub, Begley did. "The juice of the barley" he called it but he didn't seem to drink much of it himself; he sold it to the bootleggers. Begley was Irish from the other side and the old man called him a "brogue." He had a nephew whom she thought was so handsome that her heart fluttered every time she passed him on the stairs or saw him sitting up on the roof looking at the stars.

"Bastard!" shouted the old man, slamming his fist on the table.

The coins jumped in the beer and the growler rattled.

"Tryin' to jew me outta my change, you little shit!" he yelled, turning toward her brother. He pushed the table violently against the wall. The calendar fell with its blue fish and the jelly jar full of liquor jumped and smashed on the floor.

"Jesus!" he roared. "See what you made me do!"

Her brother quivered and tried to back out the door. But the old man was too quick for him: he leaped and grabbed him and pushed the boy against the sharp edge of the icebox. The boy gasped in pain. The old man raised his fist.

"Leave the boy alone!" screamed her mother, suddenly dropping her sewing.

The kitchen reeked from the raw smell of whiskey and the old man looked fiercely at his wife, his fist still raised and his

12

hand at the boy's throat. The girl had to escape. She ducked out the door and rushed up the two flights of stairs to the roof.

Huge sky. Black with a touch of red from the heat of the city. Stars multiplied as her eyes adjusted to the darkness. From the back end of the roof she could see the skyscrapers of Manhattan. Like magic towers of light they rose above the flat roofs of Brooklyn. A foxtrot drifted up the air-shaft from the McIlhennys' apartment. They had a radio. She wanted to be over there across the river amid the bright lights, dancing in some swank nightclub. She shook her hips slowly from side to side and danced across the roof, her arms embracing the warm night air. Her eyes half-closed, she pretended she was wearing slinky satin. She sat on the low wall topped with terra cotta tile and looked down into the backyards, in the rear windows. People. People at their kitchen tables. Families talking. They looked happy from this distance and she hoped in her heart they truly were. There was enough unhappiness in her own house. She could hear her father screaming downstairs and her mother crying. She could hear dishes smashing, the dishes she had washed and stacked in the drainer. Some people had their heads stuck out their windows and were looking towards her family's apartment. She felt so humiliated that she could have thrown herself from the roof if she'd had the courage. She had to escape somehow. Escape. The lights of Manhattan lost their definition and flowed into each other as tears filled her eyes. She covered her face with her hands and sobbed.

She felt a hand on her shoulder. She knew it was *his* hand. She'd hoped he'd be on the roof. That was the reason she'd run up the stairs instead of going down. Looking at the stars.

"What's the story?" he asked softly.

"My father again. Drinking."

"Is that him screaming down there like a bull?" he asked.

"Yes," she mumbled, embarrassed.

"A hard man, indeed."

"I have to get away from here," she said. She put her hands on his shoulders for support. She felt weak.

"Oh, don't be worrying now," he whispered. "Everything will be fine soon."

He patted her on the back. Her dress was sticking to her skin with sweat and she could feel the tips of his fingers so well that it was like she wasn't wearing anything at all. Suddenly she could feel the muscles of his shoulders in her hands. Strong. She rested her head on his chest as if to absorb that strength. She could feel his hands enclosing the small of her back. She pressed her body against his for protection as she heard her father bellowing below. He was slamming someone against the wall, her mother or her brother was getting it for sure. For the first time in her life she felt protected from the old man.

She pushed her head into the crook of his neck like a young animal seeking solace from its mother. The stubble of his beard on the side of his throat. She could smell nothing but his flesh and taste nothing but the salt of his sweat on her lips and the salt of her own tears. His chest rose and fell as he breathed. He was the sea at night, his eyes blue, his hair black and wavy. She pressed herself tightly against him, hoping to get as close as she could to him and as far away as she could from the old man. Their lips brushed together and they kissed. His tongue touched hers and she got this wonderful feeling, a tickle that travelled down her throat into the deep of her body. She could feel too the flesh of her nipples tightening as if she were standing in the surf at Coney Island and the cool rush of water on her thighs. . . .

She lay back and he pressed himself between her legs. It hurt at first but then waves pulsed up through her flesh and her skin felt like it was glowing. This had to be love, she thought, feeling his breath on her eyelids, on the tip of her nose, on her throat. He moved back and forth like the tide, in and out, pushing himself into that most secret place that her mother said was covered with hair because it was supposed to be hidden and not seen till she got married. The stars appeared and disappeared above her head as he moved up and down, breathing and whispering to her, kissing the shell of her ear. Her father was still roaring below but she could no longer hear him. She had escaped.

ANOTHER BEGINNING. THIS time in Donegal. Annie O'Shiel was afraid of the hill even though she was born at the foot of it. The Cloigeann was its name, grand to behold, changing with the seasons; so green in summer, red with heather at harvest time, white in the winter even when there was not a patch of frost to be found in the glen. *"Moingfhionn,"* her father's father would call it then, "bright mane." But it frightened her even more when it had frosty brows for it meant "the skull" in Gaelic and when she looked up at it she'd see the fleshless face of an ould hag the likes of Ould Úna, who was sib to her mother at two removes and had the name of milking the tether on *Beal-taine* morn, which meant she could steal butter by means of incantation and trailing a *súgán* rope through the morning dew of a farmer's field. She had a wee cabin on the side of the Cloigeann, before you got to the headline you'd meet with it. Ould Úna didn't stir from it often but to collect herbs (as she had the name of having cures) or to come down to Annie's house for a bit of crack with Annie's mother, or to get a tubful of blood for black pudding when the pigs were being stuck.

That was the worst day in the year for Annie, to hear the pigs squeal in fear and they were just like people with their pink skin and blue eyes. Och, it was like murder and her mother out jabbering away with the butcher, Seán Ó Díorma, and bringing the teacup back to the house with his bloody fingerprints on the blue Delft. The horses would be *sceiteach* that day and the beasts would be bellowing in the fields for fear death would catch them too and you had to watch them for fear they'd break out and the sheep were always terrified hiding in one gray body in the far end of the Mín Charraigeach on the side of the mountain.

The weather up on the Cloigeann was different from below and mists rose quickly out of nowhere it seemed and gathered round its brows; even in the midst of a warm summer's day it could happen. The hill would hide itself as if guarding a secret and the ould people said that the *síoganna* were active then, coursing through the mists. The *síoganna* were the hill folk, the good people, and before you talked about them you were supposed to say "What day is this?" and no matter what day it was, the other person would say off this verse:

Today is Monday.
Tomorrow is Tuesday
and the day after that is Wednesday.
Their faces from us,
their backs to us,
God and Mary between us and all harm.

Monday had power against them according to the ould people, and iron, too. If Annie's mother had to leave the baby unguarded in the house she would put the iron tongs across the mouth of the cradle so that no *síoganna* might "take out" the baby. If a child died or a young person or a man drowned, the ould people said they hadn't died really but had been "taken out" by the *síoganna*. The same was true if a beast was struck by lightning or fell down the *allt* and broke its neck; no one would eat the meat and they would bury it. Meat of that kind they called "calamity meat" and the ould ones said one time the Harkins over in Míleac ate such meat and it turned out it was the body of their own aunt Siobhán they'd eaten, who died in childbirth three score years before.

Ould Úna was convinced that Annie's sister Kitty, who had died at the age of five, had been "taken out". Her grandfather said that in such cases, when the grave was opened to put another person of the family in it, they'd find a piece of burnt wood or an old broom instead of bones and that meant what they had buried wasn't the person but a mere *iarlais*, a specter that the *síoganna* had left behind to fool people after they "took out" the person.

There was nothing to be done about the *síoganna* but to

appease them, for they'd shared the world of Ireland with the tribe of Eve and they'd been living in their underground forts since before Parthalon had set his foot on the island and he was the first person ever to do so. Theirs was the mountain crag and the rocky places, theirs the holly and the whitethorn. Their lights could be seen moving over the face of the Cloigeann at night and their music would be carried on the wind coming from it and caught in the tops of the trees and could be heard as it fell slowly through the branches like raindrops after a storm. All that you could do with the *síoganna* was give them what they wanted and not offend them. Never disturb one of their white-thorns, no matter how inconvenient the place it grew. Never build a house across one of their paths. Leave out gifts of food for them on the prescribed evenings. Even the secret powers of priests were of no use against them because they had not one drop of blood in their bodies, not the tiniest spark that would fit on the head of a pin; they were not of Hell or Heaven but immortal beings of another world entirely.

Annie was upset when her father told her that she'd have to go up the mountain to the Leitir Mhór with the sheep that afternoon. She was angry with her brother Manus for being sick as it was his job right enough and besides he wouldn't be afraid at all, always looking for birds' eggs and arrowheads and odd stones and scraps of metal. He was always finding Dé Danaan's butter in the bog, buried it was in wooden bowls looking like gold dust. And Manus would be making up a grand story to go along with everything he found, of the olden times, of Niall Naoighilleach, of ancient wars against Picts and Danes in which the Gaels got the victory in the end.

Annie made her way toward the Cloigeann with the dog, Jack, running ahead of her. She carried an empty flour sack to use as a shawl in case it rained. Up through the Miadan Buí over the stile and across the Bealach, the ancient road that arrowed straight over Ardán Donn to Cabrach. Up with her through Mín Charraigeach where she found the sheep. She went past Ould Úna's wee smoke hole, giving it a wide berth, for she was afraid the ould hag would greet her and make her call in for a sop of strange tea. The dog knew the way and herded the sheep up the path through the steep fields until he reached Leitir Mhór where he turned them in. All Annie had to do was close the gate behind them. The sheep were like one huge body as they were driven, but once closed in the safety of the *leitir* they broke up into smaller clusters until they were soon spread over the length and breadth of it.

It was chilly on the hillside and she pulled the old rough linen flour sack around her shoulders against the wind. The sun shone brightly and white clouds scudded over the glen from the west; their shadows ploughed across the green meadows and golden crop fields like black ships. That put in her head the ould tale of Bran and the God of the Sea that her grandfather would often tell her. To the God of the Sea, the salmon were like calves leaping and the waves were like treetops and the sea itself was a vast forest full of nuts and fruits. And here she thought it was the opposite, the land was becoming the sea.

There was a grand view of the sea to be had from the summit of the Cloigeann so she decided to climb to the top. This was against her better judgment for she was still afraid that a stony mouth would open in this huge skull of a hill and swallow her.

She told Jack to stay with the sheep and climbed a stony ridge till she reached the top. She looked out at the northern ocean flashing under the sun and the great salt water lochs that cut into the land on both sides of the peninsula returned her gaze with a thousand silver-grey eyes. Headlands jutted into the sea like knuckled fingers in a dark row and where the Neadh ran into the loch was Carraig Inse, standing bleakly, from whose bare height the head of Friar Giolla Dubh Mac Dónaill was cast into the sea, a martyr for the Holy Faith. On the northeast horizon she could see the isle of Siúire rising with its two breasts of mountains that had fed Deirdre of the Sorrows and the Three Sons of Uisneach fleeing Ireland and the wrath of Conchúr Mac Neasa. Deirdre had suffered all, even death, for the love of the handsomest man in Ireland, Naoise. Hair like a raven on him, skin like snow, the blood of the slaughtered calf in the blush of his cheek. It was so romantic, she thought with a sigh, her eyes on Siúire, great-breasted.

To the west were a line of mountains running from south to north—Cnoc an Aonaigh, Cnoc na hEorna, Ard na Péiste, Scealp, and the most northernly was Más na Ríona, which meant "the thigh of the queen" but not even the ould people knew what queen was intended. It was between Más na Ríona and Scealp that the Host of the Air went when they were off to raid Connacht, for the *síoganna* had wars and kings just like people had them. She could see Lochán na Bréige, like a blue eye in the high green gap, where they would stop to water their horses before the long journey. The little lake of the lie. It was here that the young unmarried fellows of the parish would go every year at Lúnasa during the Assembly of the Mountain to gather the lilies that grew in its ice blue waters. The ould crowd said the deceit of the place was in the beauty of the flowers that disguised the bottomlessness of the lake where many a young man drowned in the ould days in their pursuit. It was said some *Sasanach* landlord tried to drain the loch in the days after the Famine and a red bull came out of it roaring and sent him running and the luck was on him that he got off with his liver. It was Niall Mac Orraistín, the brother of her grandfather's mother, who was on the work party that saved him from being carried under the water by the beast. The outlines of the drains could still be seen as straight lines in the green bog.

Below her were the farms of the glen. She could see the thatch of her own house and the three other houses down in Cluain Catha, her townland, and to the north in Doire Leathan smoke was rising from her friend Nancy Mac Orraistín's house. Nancy's people had been sib to Niall but what there was of a blood relationship between the families had died out. The Mac Orraistíns kept goats as they didn't have grass for a cow and Nancy's brothers all went to the "rabble" to be hired out when they reached nine years and the three oldest ones had gone off across the sea to Alba, not with swords in their hands like the Sons of Uisneach had done but with spades for the potato harvest. Nancy's father was a hard worker and people said there wasn't a flea on any of his goats, he was that tidy. The roof of his house was always kept in good repair and the walls white-washed. Annie's people respected the Mac Orraistíns for hold-ing on to what they had, as little as it was. But that didn't matter to Nancy as far as Annie could tell; she was ashamed that her people were too poor to own a single cow and she seemed to resent the fact that the Shiels had seven of them.

To Annie it would have been a great relief to be without the seven beasts for it was she who had to get up each morning before daybreak and help her mother feed them. The beasts were particular about their bit of food and in the winter Annie and her mother had to be boiling a huge pot of water to pour on the turnips to take the chill off them as you wouldn't want the beasts turning up their noses for they were the givers of milk, the source of butter, of calves to be fattened, of manure for the fields, from their skins came leather, and from their fat, tallow, and glue came from their hooves, and from their horns came buttons and combs for the hair, and crucifixes were carved out of them.

Annie followed the silver course of the Neadh as it snaked its way through the glen bordered by dark bushes. It ran past the big house of the dreaded Captain Cadgette, the chief Orangeman of the place, on whose land no Gael could set foot lest he contaminate it with the contagion of Popery. The house was hidden entirely by trees. Only God above could see down on his roof, she thought.

The glen was dotted with *cabhails*, the wallsteads of abandoned houses, wee cabins, ould smoke holes from the Famine time and the time of the Evictions that came after it. Her grandfather said that the Peelers and soldiers would come with their uniforms and guns and they'd break holes in the old thick walls of the cabins with battering rams and they'd set fire to the thatch to make sure the evicted people couldn't be moving back in. The people would cut dugouts in the bog and live on their neighbor's charity until they could get another piece of land to work on to get the passage money.

By the number of *cabhails,* she could see that the glen must have been crowded with people in the old days. There were five times as many people, said her grandfather. It made her sad to think that they had all to leave it, going off into exile across the waves. Off to America went most of them, America that "broke many a mother's heart," as was said. America was out there beyond the sea in the west. She looked long and hard at the horizon but unlike Alba to the north there wasn't a trace of America to be seen nor of the thousands who had gone there.

Going to America was a kind of dying, for they gave you an "American wake" the night before you were to leave and all the people from miles around came to pay their "last respects" to you before you hit the road. For it might be the last they'd ever see of you, so they might as well have been putting you beneath the clay. She had people on both sides who'd disappeared down the road to Ceathrú na Cille and the American boat and were never seen again. They'd been sheepmen in Oregon and railroadmen in San Francisco and coach builders in Memphis, Tennessee and street pavers in Brooklyn and Philadelphia and they'd never come back, most of them finishing out their lives amid the strangers in strange surroundings. If it was in her lot to go she promised herself then and there that she'd bring the memory of each field with her, so no matter where she was she could look inside of herself and be at home.

As she stood thinking, a heavy mist came upon her out of nowhere just as she had always feared. Within moments she couldn't see a finger in front of her face. Her heart beat wildly.

She walked slowly down the steep hillside in the direction where she thought her sheep were. The ridge line seemed to have disappeared and the rocky soil lacked its familiar solidity. She felt as if she were losing her balance; each weathered rock felt slippery under the rough soles of her feet.

"Jack! Jack!" she called. She forked her fingers in her mouth and whistled for the dog. The whistle didn't seem to travel any distance; the blanket of cloud muffled it. She sat on a large stone and whistled again and again. No dog came running sure of sense and smell to help her. She couldn't hear Jack's bark nor the bleating of the sheep even. A fit of panic hit her. Up with her and down over the rough ground, over the heathery hummocks she went, through brambles and blackthorn, whitethorn and holly, tearing her skirt and the skin of her legs until she stumbled and slid down a narrow *seoch*, twisting her ankle under the weight of her body. She began to scream for help and even as she screamed she was certain that no one would hear her voice. She scrambled out of the *seoch* but was afraid to stand upright for fear her ankle would give way. Her ankle throbbed and her heart pounded in her ears and her throat was dry with fear. She remained om her knees and crawled in the direction of the Leitir Mhór. It wasn't long crawling till she found herself going up against the slope of the mountain; she was thoroughly confused and convinced that she'd stepped on the *fóidín mearaí*, the sod of bewilderment, and that she would wander forever without getting off the Cloigeann. She called out in the cold cloud and knew nobody would hear her. She pushed her face into the ground and began to sob so deeply that she sounded like a sow rooting and she could hear the *banbhs* squealing after her with their pink skin and their bright blue eyes just like people. She thought of the butcher Ó Díorma and his bloody fingerprints on the blue Delft cup. She thought of Ould Úna gathering blood in a bowl. She sobbed until there were no sobs left inside and then she fell asleep with her mouth in the earth.

When she woke up, it was dark. Her cheek was resting on a cold wet stone and who should be standing above her but Ould Úna herself, her face lit by the glow of a burning sod of turf she held in her hand.

"Úna," Annie asked, "did you milk the tether on us, did you?"

"Don't be talking such foolishness," replied Úna. "And what is it you're doing here yourself on the Cloigeann at this time of the night?"

"Sure I'm lost and I fell asleep. Would you show me the way home?"

"*Muise*, you're far from Cluain Catha and it's too dark to be going there now," said the old woman. "But if you come with me, I'll take you to where you'll be warm and dry till morning."

"I'll come," said Annie, more afraid of remaining alone than of going with Úna.

Úna put her arm around her, covering her with her heavy plaid shawl like a great bird of prey covering her young with her wing. They walked for a bit along a path that Annie didn't recognize. Úna led the way, stepping briskly, which surprised Annie because she was an ancient hag, stiff in the joints and frail of bone. The path took them to a high crag in which there was a door. Úna opened it and the two of them entered. There was a long hall brightly lit with fish oil lamps made of very large seashells. In the brightness Annie could see that Úna's hair was no longer grey but red as flame and there wasn't a wrinkle on her that wasn't there the day she was born. The hall led to a large room crowded with people and not one of them was speaking, which seemed very odd to Annie. As she entered Annie was given a wooden bowl of *brachán* out of a large *corcán* to eat and a wooden spoon to eat it. They sat down on a wooden form. Never had steaming *brachán* smelt so good to her in her life, with the butter melting on it and a dash of creamy milk. Annie was starving with the hunger and was reaching a heaping spoonful of the porridge to her lips when a hand appeared and knocked the spoon from her grasp. It was a tiny pale hand with blue veins in it and she looked and who did she see before her but her dead sister, Wee Kitty. And Kitty looked at her with old woman's eyes.

"*Ná h-ith sin nó cha dtig tú slán ón áit seo choíche,*" she said, pointing at the porridge, warning her that if she ate it she could never leave. "*Caith uait é.*"

Annie threw the bowl to the ground as if it were poison. The bowl echoed loudly when it hit the stone but not one of the people looked round at her, not even Úna. They were all looking towards the front of the room where there was a great fire burning and next to it sat a cauldron filled with water, the size of small boat, a *curach*. When Annie looked back at her sister, she was gone.

A short man with tawny skin came into the room and stood

26

near the fire. He had a stout rope in his hands and he fashioned a noose out of it as quick as you could turn your fist. The tawny man looped the rope over the rafter several times; he got up on a little *súgán* stool, stuck his head in the noose and kicked the stool away with his foot. He was hanging himself and to Annie's amazement not one of the people got up to stop him. She was about to do so herself when Úna grabbed her on the thigh and said, *"An rud nach mbaineann leat ná bain dó."* No harm would come to her if she did not interfere. Anything she would see that night she shouldn't talk about afterwards, according to Úna.

Another man entered the room. He was tall and yellow-haired and had a stoop in his shoulders. He stood beside the tawny man who had hanged himself and whose gasps could be still be heard along with the puckering of the *brachán* bubbling up behind her, *brachán* she could not eat even though she was starving with the hunger. The fair-haired man looked at the tawny man and Annie was thinking he was going to take him down but he didn't and what he did do was leap into the fire. And again not one of those present said a word, even those who were sitting closest and actually warming their feet by the fire. They simply watched as the man of the yellow hair disappeared little by little into the flames. Not a peep out of them, not a sigh, as he was consumed to the last bit of bone and hair.

Next came the Handsome Man. She called him that in her mind as soon as she saw him. He was not too tall and not too short and like the chiefs of old there was not a blemish on his face or limbs. He was as straight and smooth as the sally rod of kingship. Black hair, snowy skin and rosy cheeks on him. He looked out at her and when she looked into his eyes she knew that this was the man she wanted no matter what. So when he turned away and climbed into the boat of a cauldron and slid down under the water, she began to sob and the room was so still that all she could hear were her own sobs echoing in the hollow stone space. The Handsome Man slid down under the water and he held himself beneath the surface and she could see his knuckles white with the effort. He held himself under till the water entered his lungs and he was drowned. Then his fingers relaxed and his hands slid from the sides of the cauldron under the water too. She stood up and could see the bubbles of his last breaths breaking the surface like the tiny bubbles of air that floated near the lily pads in Lochán na Bréige.

"Is mithid dúinn imeacht." Úna announced it was time to go, taking Annie by the hand and leading her out of the room down the hall lit by seashell lamps with rush wicks floating in the oil of fish livers. Soon they were out the crag and down the hill to the Leitir Mhór.

It was break of day and Jack, his coat wet with dew, greeted them shaking his tail, and the lambs, mad for milk after a night's fast, were thrusting their heads greedily at the ewes' dugs. A ram that stood massive amidst the sheep inspected Annie with foolish eyes.

"I know I promised to say nothing about it but what did it all mean?" she asked.

"Och, I can tell you that," replied Úna. "Do you remember him was hanged?"

"I do, *muise.*"

"*Muise,* any child born into this world at that hour will be

28

hanged or be put in the 'lectric chair if he goes off to Chicago or the likes. And him of the yellow hair, any *leanbh* born at his hour will be burnt up by fire. And the raven-haired man. A baby born at his time will die by boats and drowning."

"I'm go'n to marry him," said Annie.

"Who's that now you're marrying?" asked Úna.

"The Handsome Man with the raven hair, snowy skinned, the blood of the calf in his cheek."

"Ach, he was but a spectre, *a chutaigh*," protested Úna. "Like a film on the eyes."

"I'll save him," said Annie, disregarding her words. "I'll save him from the water. I'll keep him from the sea and the boats. I'll learn to swim as well as any seal-woman to protect him. He'll get no death!"

"He'll get no death," she repeated. She opened her eyes and she was sitting up in her bed and looking into her mother's face.

"Time to feed the beasts, *a stór*," said her mother. "You've been dreaming."

It was dark and the rain came up the glen and was beating against the front door. She got up to feed the hungry beasts, heating up the water for the turnips in the great *corcán*. And she fed the beasts two thousand mornings more until she got to play the corpse at an American wake and went off on the boat over the water. She learned to swim while she worked for the Burkes, a rich Brooklyn family who had a large summer house at Spring Lake on the Jersey Shore, and she taught their children swimming and she'd swim a mile every day herself like the seal-woman of the tales her grandfather told her. She was so good at it and had such great form that Mr. Burke got a coach over from

Princeton to look at her and the man said she had Olympic potential and that he'd work with her. But she wasn't interested in trying out for the Olympics; she was swimming so she could save the Handsome Man from drowning for she had this idea that she'd meet him that way on the shore, him being pulled out to sea by the undertow and her saving him, holding his beautiful black head above the waves. Though it wasn't in the treacherous Jersey tide she met him, but back in Brooklyn at a dance at the Round Tower Ballroom; and she didn't recognize him at first when he began talking to her, but when they danced and she felt his body lightly touching against hers she knew that it was him. And she married him three years later when he'd gotten off the WPA and found a permanent job. By that time, they'd saved up enough to furnish a 3½-room apartment with second-hand furniture and to pay for the first baby when it came ten months later.

PEGGY WAS THE oldest of the Driscoll children. She was a few years older than Mike and his friend, Charlie Doyle, who regarded her with a worshipful awe, not having a sister of his own. Charlie had an older brother, Terry. They were the children of Annie's old friend, Nancy Mac Orraistín. She'd come out to America and married a narrowback by the name of Bill Doyle.

One day Charlie was in the backyard and he looked up and saw Peggy hanging out the back window taking in sheets from the clothesline. Her long red hair was blowing in the breeze and the sheets were billowing out like white sails and from that moment on she became his Irish pirate queen, the Gráinne Ní Mháille of his heart. Maybe he had seen too many Rhonda Fleming and Maureen O'Hara movies, too many heroines with bust darts.

Charlie was also was in love with Rosemarie Collucci, Vinnie Collucci's sister. Mr. Colucci carved headstones and kept pigeons on the roof. Rosemarie had long black hair. She was his Mohican maiden because she looked like Debra Paget playing an Indian princess. Bust darts also, this time in buckskin. Charlie used to gawk at Peggy so much that she had Mike tell him that she thought he was a creep. His heart, shattered by these words, loved her all the more. That was the way she was.

She wasn't very nice to Mike either. She used to tell him that he'd looked like a monkey when he was born, covered with black hair from crown of head to little toe. She said that he ought to have been born at the Prospect Park Zoo with the other animals. She used to make him cry when he was real little by repeating "Monkey Mike! Monkey Mike!" in a sing-song fashion, and Charlie remembered being on the stoop watching him chasing after her down Brevoort Street with balled fists and tears running down his cheeks. When Mike was older Peggy used to tell him that she wasn't really his sister at all but that she was from another planet called Farglo, which Charlie thought was a city in North Dakota. In any event she used to tell Mike she'd been sent to earth to do "research" on human beings and that one day she would return to her native Farglo and they'd never see her again. This used to upset Mike, too, even though you'd have thought—the way she treated him—that he'd be glad to see her taking off in a spaceship.

Obviously Peggy didn't feel she was part of the Driscoll family for some reason or perhaps she didn't want to be part of it. Mike never really thought about what went on in his sister's head unless he was trying to defend himself from one of her attacks. He found it impossible to think of her in any neutral fashion. He had never forgiven her for not coming to his aid when he and Charlie were being "ostracized" by Sister Admirabilis, whom they called Annapolis. He and Charlie were eight years old at the time. Annapolis caught them looking into the girls' bathroom through the screen at the bottom of the door. She put pink bows in their hair and paraded them through the girls' classes until they both broke down and cried. Mike had hoped that when they reached Peggy's class his sister would run up and save him, rescue him somehow from the nun. But she hadn't lifted a finger except to point at him mockingly along with the others, another giggling face in a sea of bobbing curls. The only girl who seemed at all sympathetic to their plight was Tiny Evans and Mike wished she was his sister rather than Peggy.

EAMONN DRISCOLL. WHEN Eamonn was little Peggy used to tell him she went to Holiday College with Wonder Woman at night when he was sleeping. She was a year older than him and had him believing it. He wanted to go with her but she told him triumphantly that there was a Girls Only admission policy at the college. She made him feel unworthy, insignificant. Eamonn went directly to God for justice in the matter like the biblical

David seeking refuge from his enemies. When Mike came along a few years later, Peggy allowed Eamonn to be on her side against this newcomer. When Peggy and Eamonn would play house, Mike would play the dog not the child. The child's part would be played by Peggy's doll, Joanie. Although Eamonn was now an ally of Peggy and no longer needed God for defensive purposes, he did not give up the relationship he had developed with this supernatural being. God after all had become his friend, his co-pilot; it was wartime. God had sent him guardian angels to be his wingmen to protect him from death and other bad things. In fact, Eamonn was even convinced that it was God who had changed Peggy's mind about him and made her see his innate worth—even if, as a boy, he couldn't be admitted to Holiday College. In his mind, Mike's arrival had nothing to do with Peggy's change of heart. It was God's work. Everything that happened to Eamonn happened because God wanted it so. The whole universe was God's handiwork and he was sitting in the palm of God's hand.

Eamonn would often build a city of wooden blocks in the bright patch of sunlight near the bedroom window and sing a joyous song to himself. One of Mike's earliest memories was of crawling over and knocking down the blocks with a kick of his still chubby legs like an a infant barbarian. He clapped his hands as the towers toppled and fell in the glorious sunlight shot through with gold motes.

By the time Mike was starting school, Eamonn was already planning to become a priest. He had great hopes for himself since his father, like Christ's, was a carpenter. On Saturday mornings, Eamonn would often play Mass in the short hall between the kitchen and the living room where Jimmy kept his work bench. Eamonn would cover it with the linen tablecloth that his father's grandmother had sent over before she died and pretend it was an altar. As a substitute for the large colorful massbooks they used in church, he would use John Mitchel's *History of Ireland*, a large book with gilt-edged pages. He'd open it to one of the engravings that were covered with little panels of onion skin, such as Brian Boramha at Cluain Tarbh, the marriage of Strongbow and Aoife, daughter of Diarmuid na nGall, Cromwell's massacre at Droichead Átha. Mike played the altar boy and Peggy would play the congregation, her head covered with a handkerchief. This was the only game in which Mike got a seemingly higher rank than Peggy, for even in play women were not allowed on the altar or beyond the imagined communion rail. For a chalice, Eamonn used an egg cup and he'd wear a long bath towel hanging down his back to represent the chasuble. He'd elevate the egg cup above his head at the consecration intoning, *"Hoc est enim Corpus Meum."* At this point Mike would get the chance to ring the shiny copper cow bell marked "Souvenir of the Mohican Trail, Catskills, New York," adding solemnity to the event just as in church.

When Eamonn would get bored with doing Mass he'd re-enact the Crucifixion and Death itself. Of course Eamonn was Jesus and he'd stand on the work bench this time and stretch his arms out against the wall of the hall. He'd wear a brown electric extension cord that he'd disconnected from the lamp in the far corner of the living room wrapped around his head to represent the crown of thorns and he'd hold one of his father's tenpenny nails in each hand to represent those nails that had pierced

Christ's palms, and he'd wear the bath towel again but this time he'd have it kilted around his waist in imitation of the loin cloth that Christ had worn. He didn't wear his pajama bottoms because it ruined the effect of the scene, so if Mike knelt down, playing one of the disciples, he'd sometimes be able to see his brother's *bodalach* hanging down between his legs and that was something he'd never see on the statues in their parish church, Precious Blood, no matter how far he crooked his neck.

Peggy regained her higher status in the Crucifixion game, for she played the Blessed Mother and wore the blue blanket with the satin border over her head and around her shoulders. She would look sad, biblical and sweet and Mike would look at her and hope that God would make her that way in real life.

When it came time for Christ to die, Mike used to put the potato pot on his head and become Longinus, the Roman soldier who killed Christ. For a spear he used the handle of the push broom.

Eamonn would then look up at the ceiling in the far corner of the hall where the rusty water stain was and he'd say in his best dying cowboy voice, "Lord, Lord, why hast Thou forsaken Me?"

At this point Mike would jab him in the side with the broom handle and he'd half-expect a mixture of water and blood to come out just like it said in the Gospel. At the same time, Mike enjoyed this role a lot because it allowed him to kill his brother in a ritual fashion. He used to wish that the Blessed Mother had gotten crucified also, because then he would have gotten a chance to stick Peggy, too. This was a fun game for Mike until one time he got bored with the role and he asked if he could play

Christ instead of Eamonn. Well, Peggy and Eamonn looked at each other like he'd suggested they eat their dog, Sparks, for dinner. Then they both broke into spontaneous derisive laughter that Mike knew came from the center of their hearts and they laughed until they had pains in their stomachs and tears in their eyes. Mike got so mad at their reaction that he wouldn't play the Crucifixion game after that even when Eamonn offered him caramels.

There was only one Christ in the Driscoll family and one priest and this latter fact was confirmed by Mrs. Collucci, mother of the beautiful Mohican maid and of the studious Vinnie, a classmate of Mike and Charlie.

One Sunday, the Driscolls, the Colluccis and the Doyles went to Brighton Beach. And Mike discovered to his great disappointment that he had the wrong toes for the high estate of the priesthood. When Mrs. Collucci saw Eamonn's feet she pointed out that, like those of her own son Vinnie, his second toes were longer than his big ones. This was a sure sign of the priest, she said, because in all the great paintings Christ was always represented with second toes that were longer than his big toes. And there was no doubt that Christ had such toes for why else would he have been painted that way? Not only were long second toes sure signs of the priesthood but boys who had them could go on to be bishops and the Pope, even. Annie was convinced of the truth of this, for as she said to Nancy Mac Orraistín later, "Isn't it the Italians who would know about such things, being as all the great artists were Italians as well as all the Popes going back to ancient times?"

So it was Mrs. Collucci who put the idea of becoming Pope

into Eamonn's head for the first time. He said not only would he be the first Irish Pope but the first American Pope; as American Pope he'd convert Russia from atheistic communism and as Irish Pope he'd bring the English back to the Faith.

Even though Mike never felt anything resembling a vocation to the priesthood, the news that his toes, which were normal in length, were shutting him out from this highest of all human states, according to Catholic doctrine, caused him enormous disappointment. Perhaps it was wounded pride on his part but, in any event, he began to pray that his second toes would grow longer than his first.

The origin of Eamonn's peculiarity was a mystery to both parents as neither they nor anyone else in their immediate families had such long second toes. Thus, Annie was convinced that God had had a hand in Eamonn's toes. In her whole life she had never felt God's presence in the world, never felt Him in church although it was God's house, never felt Him after she'd received communion even though He was supposed to be in that angelic bread. She had never seen God's face in the heavens or heard his voice in the song of birds. Any presences felt in nature had always been attributed to the *síoganna,* or to the dead, "the strong, silent ones" as they were called by the ould people. These toes of Eamonn's were the first signs of the Christian God, the first evidence of his existence she'd ever witnessed personally, although this Deity was supposedly present in Ireland for fifteen centuries before she'd come into this world, since the time Patrick had brought the Faith. For although she thought she was a good Catholic and believed in the power of rosary beads and holy water—

especially water from Buadach's well in Cluain Catha, a bottle
of which her mother would send her each year along with a
fistful of shamrocks—she had no Christian faith of the kind
her children were learning about in Precious Blood through
the Baltimore Catechism. The heart of her belief, like that of
those from which she came, was much older, going back to the
Iron Age, according to the scholars. There was nothing in it of
Heaven or Hell. There was no salvation, no sin, no devil.
There was only this world and the other world, living people
and the others. There was only good luck and bad luck and
charms and rituals to bring the one and ward off the other.
This was the bedrock of her belief above which paraded a
confused line of crazed country priests, the sons of cattle
dealers and usurous *gaimbín* men, ranting about sex, drink
and dance, on whose heels came lunatic Orangemen like
Captain Cadgette, ranting about sex, drink, dance and Popery. And if the latter had the power of the state behind them
with its putteed army and police, it was the priests the people
often feared the most, for they had secret powers and might
lay a curse on your cattle and crops. They said there was many
a roofless house in which the brambles were growing up
through the hearth that was not the work of a black hearted
Sasanach but of a black-suited Catholic clergyman.

In any event, Mike made getting longer second toes the
"special intention" of his prayers for several months running.
But there was no improvement. Nothing happened. His second
toes didn't overtake the big toes. About this time, Terry Doyle,
Charlie's older brother, was charging the younger kids like
Mike a nickel to watch him play with himself up on the roof of

the building in which the Driscolls, the Doyles and the Colluccis lived. Vinnie Collucci was always too holy, like Eamonn,
to watch such carnal activities which were doubtless sinful.
Terry used to get his boner real big and red by looking at
pictures of naked women and by pulling it with his free hand.
Mike applied the same strategy to his toes to make them bigger.
Since he wanted them big for religious reasons he looked at holy
pictures, pictures of the Blessed Mother or St. Rose of Lima or
St. Theresa of the Little Flower while massaging them. The
analogy might have been valid but the system didn't work.
Second toes just didn't possess the miraculous growing quali-
ties of dicks. Thus his second toes remained what they were,
second in length to the big ones.

THERE WAS ALWAYS a connection of limbs and religion in
Mike's case. When he first came to Precious Blood School he'd
believed that nuns had no legs. He had nuns in the first grade
and all he saw was long black skirts. It was obvious that they
weren't men but they couldn't have been women either because
women had legs. That was how you could tell a woman, by the
skirt and the legs coming out from under it. Nuns also didn't
have any bosoms as far as he could see at the time. Where Annie
had a bosom with the beauty mark over the left breast, nuns had
black cloth and a dark wooden cross with a golden Christ
Crucified on it, his right foot nailed over his left with those long
second toes, which he hadn't been aware of at the time. He
continued to believe in the nonexistence of nuns' legs until

Sister Annapolis. She was teaching the 1B class at that time, and she forced him to spend a half an hour kneeling under her desk as a punishment for talking in class. It was there under that heavy wooden desk that he discovered that nuns did have legs, legs covered in heavy black stockings that ended in heavy black shoes with ugly squat heels on them. Nevertheless it was still hard for him to believe that nuns were really women because they didn't smell from perfume like real women. They smelled vaguely soapy, like little girls, not a woman smell at all. There was more smell in his mother's handbag than in the entire convent.

It was the opposite with brothers and priests. They smelt flowery like they dunked themselves in cologne before leaving the rectory and brothers' house. His father didn't smell like that. He smelt strong and he shaved only once or twice a week. Priests and brothers were always clean shaven, no bristles, no dark growth on their chins or throats. And they didn't wear shirts and pants but long dresses that were called "cassocks." These cassocks stretched from their necks to their toes and there was a long row of black buttons all the way down the middle of them. According to Eamonn there were thirty-three buttons in all, commemorating the thirty-three years that Christ spent on Earth before he was crucified and died for our sins.

Monsignor Shugrue was the head priest, the pastor of Precious Blood parish, and he wore a black cape lined with purple satin over his cassock when he was walking around. He had the cape fastened across his chest with a fancy sterling silver clasp in the shape of the eagle of St. John the Evangelist. The pastor also wore a funny hat called a "biretta" with a purple pom-pom on the crown. To Mike it looked like some kind of licorice sundae with a maraschino cherry on top. Shugrue was paunchy and wore a purple belly band sort of like a cummerbund, and when the wind caught his cape in the airy-way between the Boys School and the Auditorium he looked like a fat vampire about to take off for Transylvania.

The kids from Brevoort Street always thought it odd that they called priests "Father" when they weren't married and didn't have children. The vow of celibacy they took forbade it and Mike always wondered about this because all the men on Brevoort, where he lived, had children. To have children was part of being a man and priests therefore never seemed quite real as men. Making children and talking about it with their friends on the corner was what men did, telling dirty jokes and thumbing through the girlie magazines in Benny's candy store. However, in school the kids were taught that the religious life with its celibate state was more pleasing to God than the married one and that there was nothing in the world greater than being a priest. The priest had the power to change the bread and wine into the Body and Blood of Christ and the power to loose and bind on Earth and in Heaven, which meant he could forgive sin. If you were going to Hell a married man couldn't do anything for you, so you'd have to see a priest and confess your sins and be forgiven. This was the awesome power that the priests had. The way Mike saw it, it was a compensation for not being real men.

·　　·　　·

JIMMY HAD THAT faraway look again. This time he wasn't floating off on the calm waters of the *góilín* with his brother, as a boy, but gliding across the smooth and highly polished floor of the basketball court. The St. Patrick's Dance in Precious Blood auditorium. Green streamers hung from the high ceiling decorated with plaster diamonds. Wine red curtains covered flat-arched windows. The wood underfoot was without blemish like the body of an ancient chieftain, he noticed, as he foxtrotted over the free-throw line with Annie, down the key and under the hoop and backboard festooned with green satin garlands. There was nothing in the world as beautiful as a good piece of wood and there was nothing as wonderful and fresh as the smell of sawdust. There was a kind of cleanness to it that never faded, as if you were working in the cool heart of an ancient forest.

> And now the woods are being felled
> and we must flee over the water
> A Sheáin Uí Dhuibhir a' Ghleanna
> you've lost your lordly rank.

Snatches of the old song competed with the band music.

Eileen Evans sat at their table, her yellow hair piled on her head in large curls. He remembered that night twenty-five years before when it was falling fragrant on her shoulders, the night when they'd made love on the roof. They hadn't touched each other since then unless their fingertips grazed when they were playing canasta. The Evanses came over at least once a month to play canasta with them or they would go to the Evanses. The Evanses had a big apartment in Empire Hall, one

42

of the large old buildings off the square, a survival from the days when there were lots of wealthy people living in the neighborhood. The building was still in pretty good condition even though there was no longer any doorman standing under its canopy.

Annie considered Eileen to be a real lady and she knew how ladies and gentlemen behaved since she'd worked many years for the Burkes in their big mansion over on Brooklyn Avenue. Eileen spoke properly unlike her brothers, Bill and Deucey Doyle, who were rough and gutter-mouthed and had terrible Brooklyn accents on top of it. Eileen always had interesting conversation. She'd talk about show business and the theater and she was a great reader, getting a book a week from Womrath's lending library while Annie herself could barely manage to finish one every month. If her daughter Peggy turned out like Eileen when she grew up, Annie told herself she'd be satisfied she'd done a good job raising her; and she was glad that Peggy was friendly with Eileen's daughter, Tiny, who had such a grand vocabulary herself that if they were all living in the ould country, the ould people would have been saying that Tiny was a changeling that the "hill crowd" had left behind when they'd "taken out" the real child. Eileen herself said that, when the doctor had slapped Tiny on the bottom in the delivery room at the Swedish Hospital, Tiny had proclaimed with indignation, "Unhand me, sir, or my attorneys shall contact you in the morning!" Surely that great vocabulary would have good effect on Peggy when she went on to the university to study nursing or teaching.

Annie wanted Peggy to do well, just like Eamonn. She was

worried about Mike, though, and she wished he'd be more friendly with Vincent Collucci, who was so studious, and less so with young Charlie Doyle, who had all the bad speech habits of his father and uncle. She was surprised at Nancy letting her boy talk so poorly.

Indeed, Eileen Evans was a fine woman to have in the neighborhood as an example to the young girls that you didn't have to be chewing gum and smoking cigarettes when you got to be twenty years old, the likes of many who stood around in front of the Joy Restaurant with their infants in their carriages, not caring about the cigarette ashes that did be falling onto the blankets and them gabbing away. Narrowbacks, most of them.

There was one thing, though, that she didn't like about Eileen and it was a thing she didn't rightly understand. It was the way Eileen looked at her Jimmy sometimes. It wasn't that look of desire women would often cast on a man, especially one as handsome as himself, and she would have understood it as Eileen's husband Frank was old enough to be her father. No, the look was different. It was as if she had a claim on Jimmy, that there was something between them. She couldn't believe that her Jimmy was going behind her back with Eileen. And when would he have the time? Working two jobs as he was. Or the energy? Sure his lids was closing down on his eyes every night at 9:30. She'd often talked to him about getting herself a part-time job at the Swedish Hospital so he wouldn't be working so much but he wouldn't have any part of it.

"Devil a man will say that I can't support me family and me alive to hear it!"

Many an argument they'd had on the subject. Sure, she asked

herself, would a man like himself that was so proud, would he be sneaking around corners after another woman? If he was anything, he was honest. Nancy was always saying you couldn't trust men when it came to sex, and that was all they had on their minds sometimes. But if there was a man in the neighborhood going behind his wife's back, Nancy knew who he was and where he was poking his horn and she had few scruples about broadcasting the tale on Brevoort Street. Sure, if her Jimmy was going behind her back with Eileen, Nancy wouldn't be long in telling her about it.

MIKE WAS SITTING next to his friend Charlie, watching his parents dance together. He enjoyed seeing them look so happy together because they'd been arguing about money a lot lately and sometimes, the way his father slammed the door on his way out after such an argument, Mike was afraid that he'd never come back, even though he mostly had the dog with him and was only going as far as Benny's candy store for the evening paper. Nevertheless, it still scared him and made all things, even his parents' marriage, the foundation of all existence, seem fragile. Seeing them out there sliding over the shiny wood, they looked so happy that he knew they'd always be together.

Bill and Nancy were at the table sitting next to Eileen but they didn't dance together. Bill was off the wagon and Nancy kept looking at him as he drank down his whiskey. He'd brought a bottle of rye, a bottle of Irish and a bottle of gin. Bill was really going to tie one tonight from the looks of it. Charlie looked uneasy. When Bill went on the booze, he'd often get violent and he used to beat up Charlie and Terry and Nancy, too. Charlie used to fall asleep in class the mornings after his father had been on a rampage. The teachers would hit him for not paying attention: they never bothered to ask why he was so tired. Mike used to get mad for his friend's sake.

Often Nancy would come down to the Driscolls' apartment when the old man was on the stuff. She came for protection but nobody ever said anything about that at all and everyone pretended that she was down on a social call. Mike felt that adults were weird when it came to things like that, always pretending things were different than they were. It was as if they were somehow forced to live out the proverbs they were always quoting; in this case, *ní bítear mar síltear,* life isn't what it seems. Sometimes Charlie would come down with her but other times he would go with his brother over to their uncle's, to the great Deucey's apartment, on the Avenue above the Brevoort Rest Bar and Grill. That was where Terry preferred to hide out until his father was himself again. They knew that they'd be safe there because the old man wouldn't dare go near his brother. One time Bill and the great Deucey had duked it out in the Brevoort Rest and Deucey knocked him out and put him on display in a garbage can out front where everybody could see him. But even before that Deucey and Bill hadn't been on speaking terms. The great Deuce hadn't spoken to Eileen either for several years. So far as Mike knew, nobody seemed to know the origin of the bad blood between Deucey and the other Doyles, not even Charlie. It was the big mystery of Brevoort Street.

Deucey was at the dance that night, at a table in the corner with Bunny Imperatore and a couple of girls, but he was making like he didn't see Eileen or Bill. Mike sort of hoped Bill would start a fight with his brother when he got well oiled. He'd never seen the great Deuce fight and looked forward to it in his heart. Of course he'd been there the day the great Deucey had hit the great homer. He'd witnessed that historic event.

The highest human state for the boys of Brevoort Street was not being a priest but being a great ball player. Even Eamonn himself would have chucked his plan to be Bishop of Rome if he could have gotten a chance to be shortstop on the Brooklyn Dodgers when Peewee Reese retired. Boys played war and ball, Chinese handball, stoop-ball, slap-ball, box-ball, punch-ball, stickball and when the weather was warm it was, of course, baseball.

Mike and Charlie would go to Prospect Park with ten or fifteen other boys several times a week to play. They would gather on the stoop in the morning with their bologna sandwiches in brown paper bags and their gloves and bats—only about half could afford them—and they would begin the twenty-block walk to the park, stopping off at the Brooklyn Museum on their way to get a drink of water, to inspect the mummies' tombs in the Egyptian Room, and to make enough noise to get thrown out by the guards. They didn't consider a visit successful unless they were ejected. The rest of the day they'd spend playing ball against themselves or other teams.

Sometimes the fields would all be taken so they'd have to challenge a team to get to play. Part of their strategy was intimidation, boasting that they were "f'om Brevoort Street," which was in a tougher neighborhood than those next to the park. Mike and Charlie even had black T-shirts with BRE-VOORT BOYS sewn on them in imitation of the great Deucey Doyle's stickball team. This intimidation never worked on kids from downtown but it worked like a charm with "rich kids." Sometimes they didn't even bother to play "rich kids." Charlie would just go up and tell them to scram or they'd get their asses kicked. If a game was going against them, Charlie would often start a fight, which would end the game on their terms. Mike always had ambivalent feelings about this kind of behavior because it wasn't "fair."

It was only the time they went out to the Parade Grounds that Mike had led the charge. The Parade Grounds were at the far end of the park and the Brevoort Boys hadn't been out there before. The huge field was surrounded by large apartment buildings with brick balconies and rows of glistening windows that no old ladies sat in with pillows under their elbows and cups of tea or small glasses of beer in their hands. Yellow and black air-raid shelter signs beckoned brightly over their cellar steps. It looked like there were a hundred diamonds to the boys; as far the eye could see, backstops behind homeplates. Awe-struck, they wandered past the diamonds and the players until they saw something that took their breath away entirely. Something they could not believe at first, could not comprehend. Boys of their own age wearing *real* baseball uniforms. They looked like miniature Dodgers. They were playing in a special field enclosed by a wire fence and they had *real* bases and chalked baselines and a batter's box and a *real* home base embedded in the red earth just like in Ebbets Field. They even

48

had bleachers on the side, which Mike and the Brevoort Boys sat on almost stupefied with disbelief.

Mike thought it was all wonderful at first that boys could have such outfits and play in such surroundings but then after a few minutes he began to feel a kind of rage in his gut he'd never felt so strongly before. He looked down at his black T-shirt with its white letters hand-stitched by his mother and it looked so clumsy, so cheap, so inauthentic in comparison with the uniforms these kids were wearing. He felt like an asshole, like a jerk, like he'd been cheated and hadn't realized it till that very moment. He looked over at Charlie and Charlie looked at him. They didn't have to say anything. Charlie smiled.

"Let's get these punks!" Mike growled. "Let's get 'em."

Up the fence and over it he went and the others after him out onto the field spitting and swinging, ripping the uniforms from the Little Leaguers' backs and sending buttons shooting into the green sod. They desecrated the straight chalk lines with their worn-sneakered feet and kicked over homeplate like it was a rock they were looking for worms under. If it hadn't been for the adult umpire, they boasted later, they would have sent those rich kids home naked and carried off the bases as booty.

If the Brevoort Boys were jumping rich kids when they had the opportunity, they themselves were getting jumped by colored kids from downtown. The coloreds would often come in small armies with up to fifty or more kids. One time they swept down over Mike and the others when they were playing a challenge game. Mike was waiting to bat and they stole his glove that was lying in the grass, an ancient chapped Joe Medwick Special with five fingers in it. His father had bought it off the junkman the previous year. He was lucky he was holding on to his bat or they'd have lifted that too.

A few months later a colored kid about ten years old put a knife to his ribs in the RKO Grant. This was just two weeks before the theater went out of business. The kid demanded a nickel for candy. Mike was shocked, and then frightened, but he toughed it out. "Kiss my ass," he said to the kid before getting up and moving to the safety of the candy counter where his friend Charlie was on line. The experience made him shake inside where you weren't supposed to if you were a hero like the great Deucey.

Mike didn't understand why the colored kids were picking on guys like him. After all, he didn't have any money. Nobody on Brevoort Street or even in Precious Blood had money.

His parents told him that he had a bit more than the colored boys did and that was the reason for it. "In the land of the blind the one-eyed man is king," they said, quoting the Gaelic proverb. Mike sort of accepted that but he couldn't see that there was any connection between what he and his friends did to the "rich kids" and what the colored boys were doing to him. After all he and the guys weren't stealing, that was dishonest. The Brevoort Boys were only pushing the rich punks around. Didn't these colored kids know that baseball gloves didn't grow on trees in Precious Blood? If they wanted to steal, why didn't they steal off of those rich punks out in the Parade Grounds? Even in religion class they said it was worse to steal a dollar off a poor man than a million dollars off a guy like Rockefeller.

.   .   .

TWENTY-FIVE YEARS, Jimmy thought, and he hadn't touched her again. Of course she'd been away for many of those years. She'd left the neighborhood soon after her brother Deucey was born. Ran off and joined a troupe of vaudevillians she did. Got away from the old man. It was there she'd met and married Frank Evans himself. He was twice her age. Another old man. Och, you could never tell with people. Frank and her had a song-and-dance act together. On the Keith Orpheum circuit they said they were. That was the best of vaudeville. Evans was an agent now but, according to Eileen, business was awful. He was at Radio City that night, one of his acts was appearing in the St. Patrick's gala there.

Eileen still was holding her shape. He wished his Annie had done as well at it. Lately she'd been getting flabby. And now she wanted to get a job. To make extra money she said. Och, wouldn't they have enough money if she managed better. He squeezed her as they danced. Putting on weight all over, he thought. If she went to work she'd be eating more for sure. Soon she'd be wearing shirts and pants and letting herself go altogether. Look at that Eileen now. What a fine body! Look at the legs on her and the way she has them folded there. Wasn't that a grand sight. Wonderful knees and, God above, can't you see the inside of her thigh. That was the tenderest meat of all.

Jimmy wondered if the old man could satisfy her. He knew he could. He had. That one night. Strange how things happened.

He hadn't really looked at her until that night and then she went away and he'd forgotten about her and the night until she'd suddenly come back with her husband and child. It was during the war she'd come back just before her brother went off to the navy to become a hero. Deucey was very friendly with her then. It was only after the mother died and Deucey came home from the war that they had the falling-out. He wondered what it was about. He imagined Nancy knew but she'd never told Annie the cause of it. Whatever it was, it had changed Deucey, for it was only after the falling-out that he'd got in trouble with the law. On the other hand, Jimmy thought it might have been the war itself that had changed Deucey. It was a terrible strain on some men, war was. A bad business entirely.

It didn't seem like it had been twenty-five years since that night on the roof. There was hardly a day had gone past since Eileen had returned that he hadn't thought of it or of her, if only for a moment. He looked over Annie's shoulder as he danced. His eyes met Eileen's. They stared at each other for several moments. Then his eyes moved down her body to her breasts and rested there for a moment before moving up again. His glance wandered lightly along the line of her throat, over the shell of her ear, curving back into the arch of her brows and down into her eyes again. He quickly got a horn, which increased in size and hardness as it rubbed against Annie's abdomen. He imagined once again the remembered softness of Eileen's breasts in his rough hands as he stared into her eyes.

"Not here, Jimmy," Annie whispered playfully, feeling that familiar hardness against her belly.

"O *a mhuirnín,*" he said sheepishly. "I'm forgetting where I am."

But he wasn't. He wasn't forgetting where he was but there was a part of him that wanted to. He wanted to be between

Eileen's legs once more, floating on the deep of her eyes, the warm sea of her body, her hair like bright seaweed about him. Salty kisses. The sea breeze at home. White sails being raised against the morning. Off to Buenos Aires. Valparaiso. Santiago. Grand boulevards with trees growing down the center of them and grand houses lining the sides of them and not a thieving *Sasanach* in one of them. Sure, the Avenida O'Higgins was three hundred and fifty feet wide, one of the widest streets in the world. Wouldn't it be grand, he thought, to stroll down a street like that with a wide straw hat and a fine-looking woman like Eileen on his arm? Without a care.

But then again, he was happy where he was. And what would he do with the likes of Eileen, an American, with grand airs? He could hardly keep up with Annie herself. And besides, he loved Annie and his children and he couldn't imagine where he'd be without them. But there was no harm in dreaming though, was there? Someday the King of Ireland's son would return to the Eastern World. He looked into his wife's eyes, sparkling with controlled passion, and felt a bit guilty. His erection began to fade.

Jimmy was a carpenter by trade. A joiner he called himself, meaning he could build a cabinet or any other piece of work without putting a nail or any bit of metal in it. It was the trade he'd learned from his father and his father from his, going back three centuries to the times when the English put the Driscolls out of the business of sea-roving. Before that the Driscolls were building boats and sailing them and that brought you back to olden times before the Saviour caught the haddock and left his fingerprints on it, back to the beginning of Ireland's history when the Gaels heard the lament of Cliona's Wave for the first time and them coming in from Spain.

Now there was no call for joinery. No one cared if you could build a town or a fleet without a *smid* of metal in them. Since the war it was all tin and Formica. Wood itself was dying. No more fancy moldings, no more paneling, Hollywood kitchens was all the rage. Whatever was streamlined was what people wanted. Anything that involved wood they called "dustcatchers." *M'anam 'on diabhal!* Devil take me!

He should have taken that job in the Navy Yard Bill Doyle had offered him. Putting down decks. It wouldn't have been very challenging, he thought, but at least the money would have been better than what he was getting now. Often he felt like he should throw it all in, and the hammer with it, and go back to Ireland, to his hometown by the sea and take over his father's shop. But what then would be the story with the children? What future? To emigrate? If only God had distributed the work evenly over the face of the globe, people could stay where they belonged and not have to be moving all over the Earth just to put food in the children's mouths.

> If the Shandon Bells rang out on Sydney Harbour
> and Donegal at Adelaide did appear,
> Erin's sons would never roam,
> all the boys would stay at home,
> if we only had old Erin over here.

He remembered that he was out of work two years when he'd first met Annie. A little job here and there and then he was working with the WPA a couple a days a week, so he could afford to take her to the movies and out for a cup of tea afterwards. He was so humiliated about not having steady work that he pretended he was working full time at a cabinet maker's. She seemed so well-doing he didn't want to lose her by way of being only on the WPA. Well, in his opinion it wasn't such a great lie for he would have been, had he the wherewithal to start a little shop up. *Muise,* he could still feel the shock of embarrassment he'd felt that time when Annie saw him swinging a pick with a WPA gang and her in that big touring car of the Burkes on her way to Spring Lake for the summer. He remembered her mouth falling open with surprise and her turning her face from him as if she wanted to see no more. Well, he wrote her a letter putting down his case exactly as it was and he heard nothing from her again until September when she looked him up at his boarding house—God bless Mrs. Callaghan for she never collected the two years' rent he owed her—and she told him that she was very flattered that a fellow like himself would lie to gain her affections.

It took Jimmy another year to get a real job and there was another year of money saving before he and Annie got married. He had the same job still at Erhardt's factory in the maintenance department and he wouldn't have gotten that if he hadn't joined the Knights of Columbus. He hadn't been to a meeting in years for he wasn't a great man for special rings and secret handshakes and the like. Fixing windows and doors, building new partitions, taking down old walls, doing wiring. It could have been worse, he thought. It wasn't full-time carpentry but at least he was his own boss more or less and he got off at 3:30

every afternoon. He had a second job at Corrigan's Lumber three evenings a week from four to seven and all day Saturday if there was call enough for it. He built kitchen cabinets, tables, doors to order. It was a great shame there wasn't enough work to make it full time. He loved working with wood, the fresh smell of it. Even the saw dust on his eyebrows or when it got in the sweaty little creases round his neck didn't bother him. It was so pure and clean smelling.

He'd worked in the building trade with his mother's brother, John Begley, when he'd first come off the boat but then came the Great Crash and that was the end of work for men without long years in the union like John. John went to work on the Empire State Building, Al Smith's White Elephant they used to call it after it was finished because they couldn't find renters for it. In any event Old John didn't live to see that for an elevator fell him in it, God rest his soul and the souls of the dead. It was when Jimmy was working on the buildings and staying with John that he'd run into Eileen. . . . Well, he'd been glad of the Crash in a way as it got him out of the building work. For two years he'd been putting down floors. It was monotonous. Och, the union got you good wages and, God bless them, they were the workingman's friend, but they never let you do the whole job. Neither did the bosses. They all wanted you to be an ant in an ant hill. They didn't want you to use the brains you were born with. It was like they wanted you to be a monkey or something. The joy of work was doing the whole job from stem to stern, from start to finish. But that wasn't how the world was anymore. They only let you do bits and pieces as if you had no sense. Sure it was an insult when you thought about it, the way they treated people like a pack of *amadáns*.

He was glad in a way that Annie had kept him from working in the Navy Yard during the war because of that terrible fear she had that he'd be hurt. He understood that they'd even put men they'd hired as joiners riveting. The idea of spending the whole day riveting noisy rivets in rattling sheets of metal had little appeal to him. Of course the money would have come in handy and his boys would have looked up to him more. They seemed a little ashamed that he hadn't been a hero during the war, gone off and joined the Seabees or something, or at least worked in the Yard building boats to fight the Japanese and the Germans. He'd built boats with his father at home, hadn't he?

Bill Doyle was always offering him a job in the Yard; he was a foreman and got many neighborhood men work there. He was a fine fella and would give you the shirt off his back if he stayed away from drink. Jimmy thought maybe it wouldn't be so bad working in the Yard, at least there'd be the smell of the sea, which he didn't have at Erhardt's. And it couldn't go on much longer the way it was. Annie was always after him about the money, about getting a new stove and bigger apartment so they could have their privacy. And she was right. They had only 3½ rooms now and he and Annie had to sleep in the living room. And Peggy was already getting to be a little woman and she should have a room separate from her brothers.

When the music stopped he and Annie returned to their table.

"Is there still work for joiners in the Yard?" he asked Bill.

"As long as the war in Korea is on, there'll be plenty of work."

Annie looked over at him with alarm in her eyes.

"That'd be cool," said Mike elbowing Charlie. "Our fathers working together."

"Fightin' the Commies," answered his friend.

Jimmy asked him the pay for joiners and he named him a figure that was twenty-five dollars a week more than he was getting at the time.

"Do you hear that, *a stóirín?*" he said to Annie raising his eyebrows encouragingly. "That's twelve hundred dollars a year more than I'm gettin' at Erhardt's."

Annie shook her head with cool yet imploring eyes as if she were asking him to drop the subject without further discussion, since he knew it would embarrass her.

Jimmy didn't take the hint.

"Och, Annie, we could move to a bigger place and get that big Caloric stove you're after."

Mike noticed that his mother was moving her head from side to side as if there was fire burning in it. She put her hanky up to her nose.

"What harm would there be in me working on a boat, woman? Sure, wasn't I was born at the sea's edge and building boats in me youth?" he asked.

Tears began to flow from Annie's eyes. She got up quickly and rushed to the ladies' room. Nancy got up and followed her.

"Is she going to be all right?" asked Eileen.

"Ah sure, the woman has fits sometimes. That's the whole of it," he replied.

"That time of the month," said Bill with a smile.

"She looked very upset," said Eileen, giving her brother a scornful look. "I'd have gone with her too but I thought I might upset her more."

She looked at Jimmy with eyes full of meaning.

"*Ara,* why would you think that?" he said with a kind of confused and embarrassed look. "Annie has great respect for you."

"I'm not exactly an old friend of hers like Nancy is," she replied. "If you're upset you don't want outsiders around. That's how I feel."

"Nancy would have followed her in, even if she was Margaret Truman," said Bill contemptuously. "Always after a story. Doesn't want to miss a trick."

"Don't be considering yourself an outsider in the Driscoll house," said Jimmy to Eileen.

"Annie had this dream when she was young," he continued. "I was in it according to her—even though it was years before we met—and I drowned in a metal boat. Well, she swore to me that she'd never let me work on a metal ship as long as she was breathing."

"Gee, I didn't know that," said Mike.

"Well, mothers don't be telling children everything, *a mhic-ó,*" he replied with an edge to his voice. "And you don't be telling her I told you, long ears."

Mike felt bad as if he'd done something wrong but he didn't know what.

"I won't say nuttin'," he replied.

"That's why she was so upset," said Eileen. "I can understand that. I can still remember dreams I had as a girl. Nightmares. My Tiny gets nightmares too."

"Well, it wasn't exactly a nightmare Annie had like ye'd be getting here. It was back in Ireland, y'know."

Jimmy gave a summary of Annie's tale of her night on the Cloigeann.

"Sure Annie's not certain yet that it all didn't really happen," he said in conclusion.

"It's all malarkey," scoffed Bill. "Nancy has a whole suitcase full of bullshit stories like that."

"There are more things on Heaven and Earth than are dreamt of in your philosophy," replied Eileen.

"Oh yeah? I don' got no philosophy," her brother answered. "All I know is that if I paid attention to every bad dream I ever had, I'd never leave the house in the morning. If you want the job, Jimmy, take it. It's yours. It's safe."

"You're right, Bill. It's all superstitions, *piseoga,* as they call them back home," replied Jimmy. "But what's a man to do when his woman feels that strongly about something?"

Bill looked at Jimmy half-scornfully and downed his whiskey.

"If yuh let broads run yuh life, yuh sunk," he said firmly.

Eileen groaned and shook her head in mild despair.

"You sound like the old man," she said, referring to their dead father.

"Yeah? An' if I do, what's wrong with that? He wasn't so bad."

Jimmy remembered the old man. He remembered his drunken bellowing that night on the roof. A devil for the drink.

Eileen didn't answer. There was pain in her face. She looked at Jimmy and became flushed as if she too were remembering the night.

Annie and Nancy returned to the table. Annie had a nervous smile on her face as if she were bracing up.

"Don't worry, woman," said Jimmy to her. "I'm not takin' the job."

Bill shook his head in a condemnatory fashion.

"Then why did you say you was?" Annie asked, relieved, and her anger coming out with the relief.

"I never did. I was just thinking out loud," replied Jimmy.

"It's punishing me he was," Annie said looking at Nancy and Eileen. "For wanting to get a part-time job at the hospital. A nurse's aide or something in the kitchen."

"That's not true at all," replied Jimmy.

"He says I'll be wearing pants and shirts next, he says," continued Annie.

Bill drank down another drink and looked at Jimmy with an I-told-you-so expression on his face.

"You don' wanna work in the hospital. That's nigger work," Bill announced.

"Och, don't be saying that word, Bill," said Annie. "It's not nice."

"It's true. Too many niggers—excuse me I mean coloreds—over there since the war, since Roosenfeld was president."

"Cut it out, Bill," said Eileen sarcastically. "My brother likes

61

to think Roosevelt was a Jew, one of the elders of Zion, don't you, Bill?"

"All I know is he put a bunch of pinko Jews in charge of Washington. Fuckin' coons—excuse me, colored people—have been gettin' uppity ever since. Back when Hoover was in, spades—excuse me, colored folks—knew their place."

"I think there's room for everyone in this city," said Jimmy.

"I agree," said Eileen. "It's a big town. A big country."

"Right you are," Annie agreed. "Sure, it's not like the Orangemen was running things, like in the Six Counties back in Ireland. If you was in Belfast, Bill, you wouldn't have that good job you have for they don't let *Papishes*—as they call Catholics—work in the shipyards."

"Well, I can't help it if they're a bunch of assholes. We should send 'em a boatload of coloreds and they'd change their tune soon enough."

"It's no use reasoning with my brother," said Eileen. "He doesn't listen. Wax in the ears gone into his brain."

"Well, my lady, how do you like that they turned the RKO Grant into a Baptist church?" asked Bill.

He was referring to the movie house on the square that had been converted into a black church only the week before.

"That means the neighborhood is going. Downtown Brooklyn is gone already. Sands Street. Irishtown is gone. The projects are gone. Myrtle Avenue. Bushwick. Queen of All Saints is gone. Our Lady of Victory gone. Pretty soon it'll be Precious Blood. Gone."

Mike listened and it sounded like these streets, neighborhoods, parishes had slipped from the face of the earth the way

Bill Doyle spoke. It was like they'd fallen into the black abyss of space and disappeared. It scared him.

"Better the building be used for some purpose than torn down," Eileen replied. "Frank and I did a show there once when we were working. Very good acoustics."

"It's got beautiful plasterwork inside. Sure it's pretty enough to be a church," said Jimmy.

"What kind of people would put a church in a movie theater? Tell me! I wonda what my brother Deucey thinks of it. He grew up in the place. He used to sneak in after he come home from school. Then he was an usher there before he went in the navy." Bill laughed maliciously. "It'll kill him."

DESPITE THE FACT that Eileen had been in show business, Deucey was the most famous of the Doyles. For the boys of Brevoort Street he was a hero, a legend in the flesh whom they could watch pitch pennies in front of Santo's Bakery. All the tough guys hung out in front of Santo's. Bunny Imp was one of them with his peg-pants and pistol pockets and his toothpick rolling over his teeth from one corner of his mouth to the other as he talked. He was Deucey's best pal and it was his grandfather who, they said, had Arnold Schuster killed for singing to the cops about Willie the Actor Sutton. Old Man Imperatore used to appear at Santo's once a week at least. He was a loan shark according to Terry Doyle. He had a large head and white hair that flowed out from under his grey fedora and a cold, hard expression on his face that made him look like God the Father to

Mike, the God who sent the Angel of Death to slay the little Egyptian babies, the God who loved Jacob for cheating his brother out of his inheritance. There was little bread sold in Santo's and where the ovens should have been in the back were tables with telephones and men in fedoras at them. It was a bookie joint.

Terry Doyle used to run numbers part time for Santo so he had "inside information," as he bragged. Santo himself had the innocent face of a child and he used to give away free lemon ices to kids during the dog days of summer. Everybody loved him. A cop car used to show up at Santo's every week but they never closed it down even though betting parlors were illegal. Terry said that the cops'd get a brown paper bag full of money that they'd bring back to the precinct captain. The cops collected from almost all the legal businesses in the neighborhood too, according to Terry. If it wasn't the cops it was the fire inspectors and the garbage men, because every business broke some kind of city regulation. Like Catalano's grocery store where Terry worked when he wasn't running numbers—their fruit stands stuck out four inches too far onto the sidewalk so they had to pay. But Old Lady Catalano was no fool and she had the garbage men collecting her garbage every day in return for their lunch. That way she didn't have to pay for private sanitation.

"Everything is a racket," Terry used to say. "The whole fuckin' world."

Terry said when he got outta the service, he was gonna be either a bookie or a cop because he wanted in on the gravy.

Mike idolized Deucey Doyle. He was everything that his brother Eamonn wasn't and his mother was always holding

64

Eamonn up as a model. Unlike Eamonn, Deucey was a man of action. The only thing he ever studied was The Racing Form that he bought every day at Benny's. He wasn't no clown either because of that. Terry said he'd pulled off some "high-class jobs" since he'd got out of prison. Terry said that the wise guys said that the Deuce had the makings of a second Willie Sutton if he got control of his temper. He was hotheaded, which matched his fiery red-blond hair.

Deucey was also a hero, something that Mike's father wasn't. When he'd got his chance to fight the Japs, he'd taken it, unlike Jimmy Driscoll. Even this latest discovery, that his father had stayed away from war work in the Navy Yard for his mother's sake, didn't really lessen Mike's disappointment. What kind of a man would listen to a woman? Not a hero certainly. He'd never seen the likes of his father up on the movie screen and never would. John Wayne didn't listen to no women, nor did Randolph Scott. They didn't have girlfriends, and if they did, they left them behind on the dock crying while they went off to attack another island. Heroes had no time for women. Bill said that Deucey had enlisted when he was sixteen; when his mother wouldn't sign the papers, he forged her signature. If Deucey had paid attention to his mother he woulda never become a war hero, he woulda never become Deucey Doyle.

Deucey was a genuine war hero. He'd been on board the carrier *Franklin* when it was hit by the Japs in the Philippine Sea. There were 882 sailors died on her, according to his pal Charlie, and if it hadn't been for Deucey, it would have been 888. The great Deucey had swum through burning oil to save six shipmates from certain death. He got a medal for that; he had a collection of them. Charlie and Mike hoped the Korean War would go on forever so they could get a chance at some medals themselves when they grew up. Charlie said the Japs couldn't sink the USS *Franklin* no how, and that Deucey and the other survivors had brought her all the way back to the Brooklyn Navy Yard. His father had told Charlie it had been one of his proudest days, watching the carrier sailing up the river under the Manhattan Bridge surrounded by tugs and fireboats blowing their fog horns and shooting jets of water into the air. And there was Deucey topside, his medals shining in the sun amid the twisted ruins of the flight deck. That was before Deucey stopped talking to Eileen and Bill, when they were still friendly, before Deucey had put Bill in the garbage can in front of the Brevoort Rest beergarden and made a laughing-stock out of him. Charlie felt ashamed every time he thought of it. Even though he hated his father sometimes for beating him up, he didn't want people laughing at him. Charlie also didn't know what the reason was for the bad blood between Deucey and his father and his aunt Eileen. Nobody would talk about or tell him. That was the family mystery and he didn't like the fact that it had become a neighborhood mystery. He figured if his father and his aunt Eileen hadn't talked to his uncle Deuce for years, that was Doyle business and nobody else's.

Annie had told Mike that Deucey must have had the three gifts of the Sons of Uisneach to have done that heroic feat in the Philippine Sea: no weapons could kill them; no seas could drown them; and no fire could burn them. They'd carried Deirdre of the Sorrows across the sea to Scotland to the island of

Siúire with its twin mountains round and full like the breasts of a nursing mother rising out of the sea. Right on the horizon you could see them, Annie had told him, if you were up on the summit of the Cloigeann. It was on Siúire that Deirdre and Naoise had spent their honeymoon, their brief time of happiness.

Mike wished that he had been on the burning deck of the *Franklin* with the great Deucey that day, the air full of crashing kamikazes, bursting flak, red glare of rockets, a sky turned into fire and blood as Colmcille had prophesied for the Great War of Erin long ago. He envied Charlie his being Deucey's nephew. How great it would be, he thought, if he was Deucey's nephew instead. He imagined how wonderful his world would become if he had Deucey as an older brother instead of Eamonn! Everybody would look up to him. All the kids on Brevoort would be dying to be friends with him.

Besides being a war hero, Deucey was a legendary stickball player. He was the best in Brooklyn and Eamonn said, if you were the best in Brooklyn, that meant you were the best in the entire world because Brooklyn was the world capital of stickball. If Eamonn said something, it was true. They didn't call him Dr. Einstein in Precious Blood School for nothing. He had all the Dodger statistics memorized going back to the Series of '41 when Mickey Owens dropped the third strike pitch.

The stickball games that the big guys like Deucey played in were held on Sunday afternoons in the summertime. The teams played for money. They'd keep the money they'd bet on the game in an upturned hat on the sidewalk in front of the statue of General Grant and it would be full to the brim with bills most of the time. The hat would stay there the entire game because nobody trusted anybody on either side to hold it and both sides wanted to be able to see it at all times so nobody would get the idea of lifting it, or a couple of bills out it, when they saw they were gonna lose.

They played two-strike, sewer-to-sewer ball and they used to block traffic if there was an important play on. They'd send Donny Muldoon out to hold up the cars. He was six foot seven and so big the army turned him down for Korea because they didn't have his size of boots and uniforms. He couldn't play ball for beans. No coordination. But he used to scare the hell out of the people in the cars so they'd never make trouble about the jam-up.

Teams came from all over Brooklyn to play Deucey Doyle and the Brevoort Boys. They were the team to beat, the best there was, like the Brooklyn Dodgers. Italians would come all the way from St. Rocco's. Coloreds up from Our Lady of Victory. Most people in Precious Blood were afraid of the coloreds. They said that the coloreds carried shivs and razors and they'd stick you as quick as look at you.

People said if the war hadn't come along and if Deucey had gone into baseball like he should have, the Dodgers would have had a slugger to put against the Yanks of the same quality as the great Joe DiMaggio. The Dodgers would have pulled out the series in '47 for sure if they'd had the great Deuce hitting for them. He was that powerful a hitter, people who knew said he woulda been sockin' so many balls over the right field fence at Ebbets Field that he woulda broke Ruth's record for sure.

There was an armory on the corner of Caspian Place, a huge

barrel-vaulted building with towers of red brick reaching up like fists into the blue summer sky. The towers looked powerful and the buildings nearby always seemed to be cowed by them. Twice a year tanks would roll out of the armory in the early morning and they would lumber over the streets through the neighborhood making the buildings shake on their way upstate to "manoeuvres," which Mike knew was a French word like "corps" and "Chevrolet" because Eamonn had told him. The armory was a block behind where the deep centerfielder played and when Deucey got up to hit on that Sunday afternoon in August, the summer before the St. Patrick's dance it was, not one person in the crowd that was gathered on the sidewalks, stoops and fire escapes to watch would have expected even the great Deucey to hit the ball so far. The clock said 3:14 in the window of Kleinberg's Laundry and Cleaners when Deucey Doyle came up to bat.

Mike was up on the pedestal of Grant's statue with his back against the cool granite and his head under the letter Y in Ulysses. Grant was larger than life and stared intensely into the distance as if expecting the enemy, oblivious to ball games. The hat, full of money, was between Mike and Deucey. But Mike wasn't looking at the dollar bills at all and dreaming about what he could buy with them like he'd often done, he was concentrating on the Deuce because the Brevoort Boys were down by two runs in the final inning and there was a real possibility that they might lose a game for the first time in two summers.

They were playing the Jokers, a team from Grand Avenue, all tough guys, some on parole and probation by the looks of them. Rocky G. was pitching for the Jokers. He was a contender for the middleweight crown and he played stickball to keep in shape on weekends when he wasn't fighting a bout at the Eastern Parkway Arena or St. Nick's or Sunnyside. People said he was connected with Old Man Imperatore and used to do jobs for him. He had the shoulders of a bull and muscular long arms. Despite this, he used to pitch the ball nice and easy, but he had a great fluke so he'd struck out a lot of guys, including the great Deucey his last time up.

Deucey wore a black T-shirt with BREVOORT BOYS in gold letters sewn across the chest. He had the number 7 on his back. Mike and Charlie were wearing similar shirts with white letters but without numbers. Shirts that Mike had been extraordinarily proud of until he'd seen the Little Leaguers out in the Parade Grounds. The shirts expressed their desire to be playing members of the team when they grew up. Then they'd qualify for the gold lettering. At the time it meant they were honored if one of the big guys sent them to Benny's for cigarettes or to Catalano's for a bottle of beer or soda.

There were two men on base ahead of Deucey; Bunny Imp was on first and Tommy the Hat was on third. It wasn't Tommy's hat they were using to hold the kitty. Tommy never took his hat off, that's how he'd gotten his name. According to Terry Doyle, Tommy was a gambler and fenced stolen goods.

It was 3:14 P.M. Mike looked at the clock again just as Deucey assumed his low crouch of a batting stance. He had a smile on his face and he shook his bat slowly back and forth like a cat wagging its tail before going for the mouse. He had the sleeves of his T-shirt rolled up over his shoulders. A blue navy anchor in a field of green shamrocks was tattooed on his left biceps and on the right he had a red heart and roses entwined around it.

People said that he used to have MOM written on a scroll beneath the roses but that it had been burnt off when he was saving his shipmates in the fiery waters of the Philippine Sea. His mother had died when the *Franklin* was making for Brooklyn after being attacked, according to Charlie, and the Deuce hadn't had the heart to have MOM re-tattooed on him after that. This proved to Mike that the great Deucey was a man of sentiment even if he was tough as nails.

Old Man Doyle, Charlie's grandfather, had died right before Deucey left home to join the service. Deucey didn't have DAD tattooed anywhere but no one would have expected that, since the old man had been a real devil for the drink and a terror. All the Doyles had been happy when the old man died, his father had told him.

Deucey's muscles flexed when Rocky G. released the pitch. The long, thin broom handle of a bat met the pink rubber surface of the Spaldeen. Mike heard the wood cutting through the humid August air and the clear pop of the ball as it was struck. It'd sounded bright and pure like a fiddle string being plucked before one of those big Kerry reels, shivering delight into the legs of the dancers. There was childish glee on Deucey's face as the Spaldeen streaked off in a high rising arc. Like a shot it zipped past General Grant on his horse. It became a rapid pink blur against the true blue of heaven. Above the straight roof lines of the buildings, above the rusty metal cornices of the tenements it flew.

All eyes turned up, all necks bent back, like the disciples in holy pictures watching Christ ascending into Heaven. Everyone frozen on stoops, on fire escapes, on sidewalks of blue slate, on curbstones, in gutters, on grey metal manhole covers, on car bumpers, on chrome fenders. No one and nothing moved but the pink Spaldeen. Up, up it went, higher and higher, higher than the six flights of the Empire Hall with its fancy brickwork, with its dark lobby of heavy furniture and ancient elevator where the Evanses lived. The ball out-arched the arches of its windows and for a moment Mike believed that it was zooming toward eternity. Suddenly, it began to fall and a sigh rose up to meet it out of the open mouths and the throats, relaxing, and the thankful lungs that could start breathing again since the Spaldeen was indeed returning to Earth. But still no one moved and the crowd watched as the ball arched downward toward the ground. It struck the armory, one of the tall red brick fists, struck it on a fly. People gasped in disbelief. No one in the history of Brevoort stickball had ever done that before.

The ball bounced off a ledge and went careening off down the avenue with the centerfielder chasing after it. It ended up zipping right down the sewer on the far corner like a pool ball in a pocket. That didn't matter since, even if he had caught up with the ball, Deucey could have walked the bases by the time the throw reached home. There was so much shouting and applause for Deucey that he had to run the bases again as an encore and even Rocky G. and the Jokers from Grand Avenue, even they clapped hard for him and whistled their appreciation. It was an historic moment. Three runs had scored and the Brevoort Boys had won another game.

While the crowd was swarming around Deucey, Eamonn

Driscoll took the opportunity of getting Rocky G.'s autograph. He had the boxer sign the margin of his Classic Comic, "The Deerslayer." Afterwards he ripped the margin out and kept the autograph in the base of his statue of Our Lady of Fatima, which he'd won for getting the highest marks in religion. It read *Good Luck, Rocky G.*

After the excitement was over, Deucey offered Charlie and Mike two-bits each if they could salvage the Spaldeen from the sewer because he wanted it as a "silvernir," as he called it. Charlie wrapped a wire hanger around the broom handle and they searched for almost a half hour through the murky corners of the sewer, not coming up with anything but last year's rotting leaves and a collection of ice-cream pop sticks. Charlie figured that the ball had probably gone down into the main sewer and was already on its way to the harbor. Mike said it probably would end up in Coney Island and some clown, who didn't even know how important it was, would grab it off a breaker and bring it home. They were very disappointed that they couldn't find it and so was Deucey because he wanted to get it mounted and hung over the bar at the Brevoort Rest where he did most of his hanging out at night.

The next day Mike got his father's six-foot measure and he and Charlie measured off the distance between home and the spot on the armory where Deucey's home run had hit. It was 580 feet to the wall and about thirty feet up to the ledge where the ball had hit, which made it 610 feet and it would have been more had the wall not been there. Eamonn went along with them and said without doubt it was the longest home run ever hit in the history of Brooklyn stickball, which meant it was the

73

longest stickball homer ever hit anywhere because Brooklyn was first in the world in the game.

The Spaldeen was never found and because of that it became even more important for Mike and Charlie than it would have been, had it been found and mounted in the Brevoort Rest. It became one of the neighborhood intangibles. It had entered that mythic space into which heroic movie characters were assumed as the words THE END spread out across the screen and the curtains closed.

Charlie made a signal to Mike to follow him as he got up from the table. He told Nancy they were going to get some fresh air but what he really wanted to do was talk to his Uncle Deucey. The boys pushed their way across the dance floor to the side door of the building. They stood in the windy airy-way between the auditorium and the Boys School for a few minutes inhaling the sharp March breeze, then made their way back inside through the thick crowd to his uncle's table. Deucey and Bunny were drinking shots and beers. The women they were with went to "powder their noses" so Mike and Charlie sat down. Charlie asked his uncle what he thought about the black church moving into the RKO Grant.

"I didn't fight no fuckin' war so no niggers could take over no RKO Grant," Deucey declared. "This is fuckin' America, ain't it?"

"Nigguhs is tryin' to take over Brooklyn," said Bunny Imperatore. "They got this church. Next thing they'll have the neighborhood."

"When I think how many great movies I saw in the RKO. Gable, Garbo, Cagney, Ramon Navarro, H. B. Warner, Edward

G. Robinson, Nelson Eddy and Jeannette MacDonald . . ." said Deucey.

"Fred Astaire and Ginga Rogers, Betty Grable, Bogart, Bela Lugosi, Peter Lorre," added Bunny.

"When I think of all the great ones and then niggers sittin' in our seats, fuckin' jungle bunnies!"

"Dad said you was an usher there before the navy," said Charlie.

"I still got my usher's uniform. Man, was I proud of that? Hey, when you guys is a little olduh and wanna make out wit' the ladies, that usher's uniform woiks like a charm. Broads, they like uniforms. Navy. Marines."

"Except cop uniforms," added Bunny.

"Right, no flatfoot uniforms," replied Deucey.

"It ain't right for nigguhs to be fuckin' around in this neighborhood," said Bunny. "They gotta stay where they belong, like downtown. We ain't trying to push 'em out where they are, so why they tryin' to push us out?"

"Right, Bun. This is America. Evvybody's got their own place; whites with whites, spades with spades. That's the way it is, even in jail it's like that. Right, Bun?"

"Fuckin' right. Whites in one cellblock, coons in the other. No mixin'."

"Listen, boys, I'll tell you a story I ain't tol' too many people, about when I was in the jernt."

Charlie and Mike were all eyes and ears.

"Like they got five ballfields in the jernt. Four of 'em for white guys and one for nigguhs," began Deucey. "The way it's set up, no nigguh can step on no white field no matter what, an' if he does, his ass is handed to him. Get me? One day I'm up at bat and it was a real important game. The playoffs it was and evvybody's dependin' on the old Deuce to put one away."

"Tommy the Hat says you got yourself sent up just so's you could play inside, just in time for the opening of the Sing Sing baseball season he says," interrupted Bunny Imp with a laugh.

"You know me. I'll go anywhere to play ball," replied the Deuce. "Well the count was 2 and 2 in this here game and what happens but this fuckin' jig comes running over on our field chasing a foul pop. Well, there he is and there I am. I got the bat and he's lookin' up in the sky after the ball."

"What you do?" asked Charlie.

"Tell 'em what you did, Deucey," said Bunny. "Tell 'em what you done to the *mulignan*."

"Well, the pitcher truns one down the pipe. What I coulda done with it. But I didn't hit it. I zonked the nigger instead. That's what I done! I hit the fucker till he went down. Scumbag. I coulda had a double or a homer but I wasn't thinkin' about my battin' average 'cause I'm a stand-up guy an' I done what was right."

"You wanna be a stan'up guy, you gotta ack like a stan'up guy," said Bunny. "You hear? That's what it's all about, boys."

"I got the hole for what I done. Thirty days in solitary. And evvy fuckin' Saturday night the screws used to get juiced up and they'd kick my fuckin' ass 'cause they don't like no guys from Brooklyn. They don't like the Irish. They don't like Italians. They hate fuckin' Jews. Scumbag fuckin' hicks!

Thirty days. I done it standin' on my head 'cause I'm a fuckin stan'up guy."

He laughed at his own unplanned witticism.

"You seen this scar, ain't yuh, Charlie?" asked Deucey.

He opened his shirt and showed the boys a long slash of a scar under his left breast. It was the very same spot that Jesus got stuck by the Roman soldier. Mike figured if Jesus had recovered, he would have had a scar just like Deucey's. Nasty and ugly looking.

"Feel it," he said.

"Gee, that musta hurt," said Charlie.

"Be my guest, kid," said Deucey, motioning to Mike.

Mike touched it with respectful fingers, remembering the story of Doubting Thomas.

"I didn't get this in the war like people think," said Deucey. "I got it in the jernt. Nigger gave it to me. It was in revenge for zonkin' the coon who come on our field. It was six months later. They cornered me in the terlet. I forgot all about that coon but the coons didn't. Fuckin' niggers don't forget shit."

"What we gonna do about the niggers in the RKO?" asked Bunny. "Bedford Christian Church it says on the marquee. What kinda name is that for a church? Those fuckahs got no saints?"

"Protestants don't have saints," said Mike.

"Yeah? How do you like that! If it wasn't for Saint Ant'ny, I'd be dead. When I was a kid I had a fever so bad they thought I was goin' for sure. They had me down the hospital, gave me the last rites. But my mother prayed to Saint Ant'ny, so I'm alive.

Every year she makes a novena over Manhattan to him. So the *mulignans* got no saints. How do you like that? Church in a movie house. RKO Heaven! Y'get that, Deuce? RKO Heaven?"

Bunny burst into laughter.

"But we're gonna make it RKO Hell for them!" he said, continuing to giggle. "Ain't we, Deuce? Ain't we?"

"That's right, Bunny boy. We'll get 'em out if we gotta burn 'em out."

Both men were laughing. Charlie joined in.

Mike smiled because he thought it was expected of him. But he was shocked by such talk. He hoped it was the whiskey talking. Mike's parents wouldn't allow words like "nigger" or "coon" to be used in the house. They explained that every nasty thing the white people said about the colored people in America was said by the *Sasanachs* at home about the Gaels. That Irish-Americans could say the same things about blacks as was said about their parents and grandparents and with the same vicious hate was one of the sorrowful mysteries of America.

"'*Clanna ríthe, maca Míleadh, dragain fhíochta is gaiscígh,*'" Jimmy would quote. "'We are the children of kings, we are the Sons of Milesius, fierce dragons, champions.' And look at the terrible fate that befell us in Fodla's noble plain; reduced to tenants on our land, slaves, *seoiníní* toadying about, licking the *Sasanach* boots. And if you stood up, they hanged you just like they hang those colored men down south in this country. Oh, I tell you, *a mhic-ó,* no one's born to slavery and it's not just us Gaels who have the blood of kings. Every man has the blood of the kings running through his veins. Different kings for different tribes. The kings came out of the people.

"*Ara,* they talk about the common people and the common man; *muise,* I've never met one. People is uncommon, sure that's what makes them, each person, what he is, different, interesting. It's the same case with wood, each piece is different from the other even if it's from the same tree. Och, when a man of Irish blood is givin' out about 'niggers,' it's like he's calling himself a nigger. He's spitting in his own face."

It was easy to accept what his father said in the almost Gaelic world of their kitchen, it was another story on the American street. Mike didn't want to be called a "nigger-lover" on the street. He didn't want that reputation because it would have meant he was different, and if you were different on Brevoort Street it meant you couldn't be trusted. You were out. You would never be let in on what was really going on. Charlie Doyle would not have been his friend and he'd have never got to touch the great Deucey's wound. And beside what had the coloreds ever done for him except steal his baseball glove and put a knife to his ribs?

THE FOLLOWING SUMMER, Mike stood in the square. The marquee of the RKO said WE PREACH CHRIST CRUCIFIED AND RISEN AGAIN in the same lettering they'd used to advertise the movies that were playing. He thought it was weird. General Grant hadn't changed. He was still up on his green bronze horse. He was green bronze too, twice life-size. He was wearing a "calvary" hat and a long "calvary" coat and Eamonn said it was the outfit he'd worn at Spotsylvania, in the Wilderness, at Bloody Angle. He'd lost seven thousand men in thirty minutes there, according to Eamonn. Four men every second. They died "to make men free," according to the "Battle Hymn of the Republic," to free the colored people from slavery.

A truck came hurtling through the square past the general, its canvas tarpaulin flapping. It braked sharply and turned into Green Street. A large piece of linoleum carpet fell out of the back. Mike could scarcely believe his eyes. Quickly he leaped out into the street and pulled the carpet back on the sidewalk. His first thought was of the carpet gun that he had hidden in the cellar of his house. There was at least a thousand "shots" in this one piece of linoleum. He'd have to hide it before any of other kids saw it.

He got on the scooter and attempted to pull the carpet behind him with his right hand while he steered with his left. He couldn't manage; the scooter was wobbling dangerously. He parked the scooter outside Kleinberg's and hoped no one would steal it while he was taking care of the linoleum. There were kids around who'd steal anything that wasn't screwed down. There were kids in school who'd steal your pen even if they knew it was the only one you had or that it was a Christmas present. Even kids that had more money than you had, they'd steal your pen, too. Sneaks. The worst people in the world, in Mike's opinion.

He hurried the carpet to the building, pulling it after him. Down the cellar he went and back through the dimly lit, coal-soaked air to the lumber room where he tore it into four large pieces. He hid three of the pieces behind a barrel and the fourth he tore into small squares as ammunition. He found the carpet gun where he'd hidden it behind an old barrel in the corner: a length of wood, a couple of nails, rubber bands and a clothes pin that would send ragged squares of linoleum shooting into the air.

But this wasn't the only thing hidden in the cellar. Mike had seen the great Deuce going down the cellar one afternoon so he'd snuck down after him to see what was up, since Deucey didn't live in the building. He'd watched Deucey move an old dresser that Jimmy had put down there with a view to restoring and refinishing it. He removed a brick from the wall behind it, put his hand in the space and pulled out a piece of rag, then he opened his jacket, wrapped the rag around something dark and put it back in the hole before replacing the brick and the dresser. Mike hid until Deucey had left the cellar, then he moved the dresser and the brick and opened the rag that was oily to the touch and found a black metal pistol inside of it. Mike's heart had pounded with both excitement and elation. It was if he had found the Holy Grail itself. He shared a secret with the great Deucey that made Mike feel a part of Deucey's world, even if Deucey himself was unaware of it.

Mike stuffed the ragged linoleum bullets in his pockets and ran back to the square. The scooter was still there. He jumped on it and sped off, feeling too old to shake the wooden weapon over his head like he used to do, pretending to be Crazy Horse or Cochise on his way into battle. He was at the age where he'd become concerned about what people would think.

He knelt behind Kleinberg's truck, its roof piled high with

bags of laundry. He hadn't used the carpet gun in a few months so he wanted to begin with a stationary target. He pretended he was a Confederate corporal at Bloody Angle and took aim at Grant. Before firing, he glanced over his shoulder at his reflection in the front window of the laundry and set his chin in a firmly heroic manner. He started firing at the general's boot and worked his way up his bronze body until he was banging shots off Grant's hat with its wide shadowy brim. He wouldn't deliberately shoot at the horse for it wasn't decent to torment horses, even bronze ones. His mother always said there was nobility in the horse and the Shiels would as soon as eat a person as eat a horse. They buried their horses when they died, like they were friends, for there was in fact no greater friend to a farmer than his horse.

He wanted something more difficult to hit, a moving target. He began shooting at the hub caps of passing cars and trucks. This was a different story. He had to estimate the speed of the approaching vehicle and the curving path of his shot. He fired off at least ten shots before he hit his first hub cap; after a few more minutes' practice he was hitting one every other shot. When he hit three in a row he paused and posed heroically once again and looked for his glorious reflection in the window of the Kleinberg's Laundry but the sun had slightly moved along its path and there was no longer any reflected image of him but only the sight of seven washing machines shaking with soap and Mrs. Tierney, from 907 Brevoort, with curlers in her hair, smoking a cigarette and reading a newspaper as she waited for the rinse cycle to add the blueing. Despite this vision Mike still felt heroic and he continued to fire.

The enemy was now the Nazis and the glittering metal hub caps were German helmets. When he struck one of them, he imagined a finer noise than that which was actually produced, a bright clear note of mortal combat that to his ears echoed throughout the square high above the rapid beating of the automobile tires as they bounced over the cobblestones.

Mike was riding high with joy when a large red hairy hand grabbed him on the shoulder. He turned his head and saw a blue uniformed sleeve. The arm of the law.

"Gimme that," said the policeman.

He towered above Mike and had red hair not only on the backs of his hands but flaming out from under his cap with the silver shield. The cop took the carpet gun from his hands and laid it on the curbstone. He raised up his foot above it. It was the biggest foot and the biggest black shoe that Mike had ever seen.

"Please don't break it, Officer. I ain't done nothing wrong."

The cop stomped down on it and the wood shattered in several jagged pieces.

"What would happen if you hit a driver in the eye with a piece of that carpet and he lost control of his car?" asked the cop.

"I didn't hit no driver," said Mike, angry and contemptuous. "I'm a good shot."

"Listen, wiseguy. If I catch you at this again, I'm gonna run you in. Get me?"

Mike looked down at the remains of his broken gun and remained silent.

"Hear me?" asked the cop, threateningly.

"Heard you," said Mike.

"Okay then. Stay outta trouble. And clean up this crap." He pointed at the splintered gun.

The cop began to walk away.

"Flatfoot," muttered Mike between his teeth.

"Say somethin'?" the cop asked, turning quickly on a huge heel.

"Who, me?" asked Mike with a mixture of pretended innocence and defiance. "I didn't say nuttin', Officer."

"You're lookin' for trouble and I'm just the man who can give it to you. Officer O'Ruarke is my name. So watch out, you little snot nose."

The cop walked away again. This time Mike said nothing. He looked down at the broken gun. His day was in ruins.

He rode his scooter around the corner onto Forest Place. It was cool and dark, another world from the bright sun and store windows of the square. Townhouses on both sides of the street, the color of brown sugar. There were no tenements with fire escapes on the front of them like on Brevoort. Even on hot days no one sat on the stoops on this street. They had backyards. This was the street of "the Sunday men," men who wore Sunday suits every day of the week and they weren't going to church either. That's how they went to work. Suits, ties, white shirts. Lawyers, doctors, businessmen. Mike thought these people were rich. That's what they were called on Brevoort Street: rich people.

As befitted its name, there were huge plane trees with ever-peeling barks that bathed Forest Place in deep shade. There were places on the street where the sun never reached at all, stoops and facades with fancy carved portals that were covered with green moss.

There was half-dead tree on the block and Mike looked up at its bare branches with great sympathy, feeling like he had lost a branch, an extension of himself, in the wooden gun the cop had destroyed. There were lots of trees dying in the neighborhood. Charlie said that the Communists were killing the trees. This didn't sound so crazy, for it was the great age of spy trials; it was the time of Alger Hiss, of Judith Coplon, of Klaus Fuchs and the Rosenbergs.

And there was Colonel Abel of the NKVD who'd been caught smuggling atomic secrets out of the country. He'd had a camera store as a front right across from the Ex-Lax factory, one parish over from Precious Blood.

Joe McCarthy was saying there were 312 "known Communists" in the State Department and, even if he was exaggerating, there had to be some there, most people on Brevoort Street thought. His parents believed him because his name was McCarthy and it was the Mac Carthaigh who had built Cashel a thousand years before and it was still standing, the royal line of Munster they were. Great people.

In any event, Charlie Doyle was sure the Commies were digging their way in from China since Truman had sold out Chiang Kai-shek. If you dug a hole in China right through the earth you'd come out in Brooklyn, Charlie said, because Brooklyn was on the exact opposite end of the world from China. The Commies were digging their way in and the tunnels they were using were killing the roots of the trees. They had underground cells down there that the spies and saboteurs used for hiding in. They could connect up with the sewers and the subway and the Edison company tunnels. They had cameras so small they could hide them in matchbooks and they took pictures of the ships in the Navy Yard. It was those kinds of cameras Abel had had in the back of his store.

The Reds were trying to get their hands on the Secret Naval Codes that were kept in secret vaults in the Yard, too, according to what Bill Doyle had told him. The codes were written in Navajo because nobody knew that language except Navajos, and the Navy had got a whole tribe of them in uniform just to do this code work. There were no Navajo Commies. But there were lots of Jewish Commies. Commies mostly had big noses and wore glasses like Jews. The Kleinbergs could be Commies according to Charlie and they could be getting microfilms and secret messages and stuff in the dirty laundry from spies.

The Commies were all basically the same according to Charlie, whether they were Russian or Chinese Commies. They were all against God and America. MacArthur was fighting the Chicom Commies to save God and the USA in Korea. As far as the Koreans themselves were concerned, the Southerners were good and the Northerners were evil. They'd become Commies after World War II; until the war, Korea had been called Chosen and occupied by the Japs. It was all very confusing to Mike.

Jimmy said that it was the Brooklyn Union Gas Company that was killing the trees. The gas lines were breaking and suffocating the roots. Mike'd asked Eamonn his opinion about the trees and his brother had agreed with their father, because even if the Commies were against God and America—which was true—it was impossible for them to be digging a tunnel from China to Brooklyn since the center of the earth was molten lava like came out of Mount Vesuvius in Italy near Naples where Mrs. Collucci's mother had come from, also the home of pizza pie, which Mrs. Collucci gave Eamonn on a regular basis to keep him strong and healthy until he'd become a priest.

In any event, according to Eamonn, the earth was like a large pudding with a skin on it, which was still boiling hot on the inside. There was no way that Commies could dig a tunnel through it. Besides, his brother maintained, that was where Hell and Purgatory were, in the center of the earth, where people had to serve out their sentences for the sins they had committed here in this life.

The earth, said Eamonn, was like a huge Spaldeen covered with dirt and water that God had sent flying into space on the day of Creation. It was shooting though the dark, dancing and spinning through the black night of eternity. Eamonn said that it spun always on its axis and that there was no such thing as "up" or "down," "above" or "below." There was no "back" and no "forth," no "under" or "over." They were all "optical illusions." The only thing holding our feet to the twisting earth was the force of gravity. Gravity was God's mercy keeping us from falling into the great emptiness. And if God changed his mind about mankind and stopped loving us, then we'd fall off the face of the earth lickety-split. That was the reason why Christians had to keep praying, to keep God loving mankind so that the world would stay the way it was until the Day of

Judgment when Christ would come again in glory and sit at the right hand of the Father.

The thought that Jesus was coming to judge him with His Father, who kept looking like Old Man Imperatore in his mind's eye, frightened Michael. That the earth was traveling through space and all that was holding them on to it was gravity, which you couldn't feel or see, terrified him. He looked up through the bare branches for a merciful face in the heaven and saw none. Suddenly, he could feel the earth turning under his feet and he was convinced that he was losing his foothold on the face of the planet, was starting to fall into the deep void behind the blue of the sky. He grabbed at the dying tree for support, wrapping his arms around it and pressing his face to it.

"Do you have nightmares?" asked a girl's voice from behind him.

He let go the tree and turned. It was Tiny Evans. She didn't have yellow hair like her mother but dark hair, and she had dark eyes to go with it, the color of mahogany. She looked like her father, they said, before he got old and gray like he was.

"No," Mike replied. "I dreamt Dracula was after me once, though."

"When I'm frightened I hug a tree," said Tiny. "It makes me feel peaceful. That's what I thought you were doing."

"I wasn't scared," replied Mike, lying. "I'm tough. I wasn't huggin' no tree. I was just seein' if I could get my arms all the way round the bark."

"Oh, I understand," answered Tiny, not believing him.

"What kinda nightmares you get?" he asked.

"I don't get different ones. I get the same one all the time."

"Jeez, that's bad! What happens in it?"

"Do you really want to hear?"

"Sure."

"I'm much younger in the dream," began Tiny. "I'm small. I'm walking with my parents. They're on either side of me and I'm holding their hands. The sun is shining and we're all smiling and laughing. My father's dancing. He's dancing up the sidewalk, up the fenders and hoods of cars, up the front stoops. He's dancing up the sides of buildings. He's dancing over the roofs and up into the sky. He's happy. We're all happy. We're whistling. It feels like Sunday and I'm wearing a party dress. I think we're on the way to the Botanical Gardens to see the flowers, the cherry trees are in blossom."

"Boy, I hate that—going to the Botanix with my family," said Mike. "Gotta dress up."

"Well. I like to dress up and besides it's a dream. It's my nightmare and if you want to comment about it, I won't tell you any more."

"I didn't mean anything," replied Mike. "Go on."

"We're going along to the park or the garden and we're all happy and then, suddenly, I feel the clown's eyes on me. You see, Mike, there are two clowns, the Sad Clown and the Smiling Clown, and I know the Smiling Clown has a long silver knife and he wants to kill me. He's following us along the sidewalk but I'm the only one who can see him. I keep crying and warning my parents that he's after us but to no avail. They just laugh—like the clown. He has long legs and big floppy shoes that beat on the sidewalk with a hollow thump. He's walking faster than us and catches up with us. I can hear his breathing behind me, over my shoulder. He has a long knife and he lifts it up above the back of my head. I can see it flashing in the sunlight.

"I struggle to break free from my parents but they keep holding my hands and laughing and they tell me I'm silly to worry. They can't see the knife although it's glittering in the sun. The Smiling Clown is about to plunge it into my back when a burst of wind comes up as we round a corner and it blows the clown's hat off—he's wearing a black bowler—and he has to stop to pick it up and my parents keep laughing and walking and I try to make them hurry because I know the Smiling Clown will come back again but they keep telling me not to be alarmed.

"And the clown does come after us again as I knew he would. His legs seem to get longer with each step he takes and I know there is no escape and his knife glitters in the sun and he's right behind us again and his arm goes up again and I can feel his breath on my hair. The knife glitters and flashes and he plunges it into the nape of my neck and just then I wake up."

"Och, scary!" exclaimed Mike. "And you get this every night?"

"At least once a week."

"And what about this here Sad Clown? Where's he?" he asked confused. "Can't he help you?"

"He's not in the dream," she replied.

"So where's he?"

"He's on the living room wall over the sofa. You know, in

my house there's a painting of a clown. That is the Sad Clown."

"I know the picture. He's got a big red nose and bells on his hat, right?"

"Exactly. The artist did a matching picture called the Smiling Clown. My mother put it away in her closet because I was afraid of it."

"And he's carrying a knife in the painting? Some kinda clown."

"No, not in the painting, silly boy. He's carrying a noise-maker in the painting. You see even though the clown is smiling, he always frightened me. The first time my father brought the paintings home, I liked the Sad Clown but the Smiling Clown made me cry. You see, Michael, there was a coldness in his eyes. Now I know it was the coldness of the knife. There's a knife inside his smile."

"Weird," said Mike with conviction.

"The man who painted the clowns was one of my daddy's acts. He was in jail when he painted them. The reason was that he'd killed his wife and the man with whom she'd been running around. He was Rodolfo of Rina and Rodolfo. His wife was Rina and the man he killed was an acrobatic dancer. My daddy used to visit Rodolfo in jail. That's how he got the paintings."

"This here Rodolfo used a knife on his old lady, did he?" asked Mike trying to sound tougher and older.

"Yes, he did."

"Well then, that's where you got the knife in the dream, right?"

"I guess. But do you know, I was terrified of the picture even before I ever heard the story. I knew there was something evil in the eyes."

"Weird," said Mike again with conviction.

"Gee," he continued after a pause, "I wonder if your Uncle Deucey knows this here Rodolfo from the jernt."

"I don't think so. He hanged himself before my uncle went to prison."

"Yaaah! Maybe it's Rodolfo's ghost in your dreams or something."

"Maybe. Sometimes, I can still feel the smiling Clown's eyes staring at me through the wall of the bedroom closet, especially late at night when the house is quiet and my father is out at work."

"Why don't you get your parents to throw the painting out?"

"My father refuses to do it. He says Rodolfo was his friend and he painted the paintings with me in mind. Rodolfo thought I'd like clown paintings because I was a child. My father and mother argue about it sometimes."

"My parents argue about money," said Mike. "My mother says we need more of it and my father says that we have enough if she managed it better. It's the same argument all the time. It gets me. I can't understand grownups sometimes. Argue about the same thing over and over."

"My parents argue about everything," said Tiny.

"Do your parents sleep in the same bed?" she asked after a pause.

"Of course," said Mike. He could feel the blood rushing to his face without knowing why exactly. "Their bed's in the living room. My mother says if she had a part-time job, we could get a bigger apartment and they'd have their own bedroom. The same with Peggy. You know she sleeps in the same room with me and Eamonn and she's getting too old for that, according to my mother."

Again he blushed.

"I don't sleep in my bedroom," said Tiny. "I sleep in the same bed with my mother and my father sleeps in the guest bedroom by himself. My mother says it's because he works late. She doesn't like to be alone."

"You don't sleep in your own bedroom?" said Mike. "Weird. At least you got one, though. Wish I had my own room."

"I don't believe her," said Tiny, disregarding his comment. "Even nights that my dad isn't working, he sleeps in the guest bedroom. I don't believe he's very happy about that. They argue about everything. My parents are sad. I wished they'd get happy like in my nightmare. It's odd that they're happy together in my nightmare. I think that's the reason I continue having it. So that I can see them happy together."

Tears formed in her eyes and began running down her cheeks.

"Ah, c'mon," said Mike, "don't be cryin' now."

He scratched his head in confusion before patting Tiny on the shoulder. Tiny rubbed her eyes and walked over to the great tree that was dying from gas or communism and put her arms about it. She closed her eyes and pressed her cheek against the peeling bark. She hugged it with all her might.

"It's still alive," she said. "It only looks dead. I can feel the sap rising through it."

She closed her eyes and hugged it again. The pain left her features and the tears stopped rolling down her cheeks.

"Put your arms around it, Michael," she said. "Feel the life."

He stood on the opposite side and reached around the bark. His arms were a little above Tiny's and the edges of their pinkies touched.

"Squeeze," she said, "and close your eyes."

He squeezed and closed his eyes.

After a long silence she said. "Can't you feel it?"

"Feel what?"

"The life," she said. "The life in it."

He could only feel the touch of her pinky and the scratchy bark.

"Can't you hear the voice? Every tree has two voices. The outside voice that one hears when the wind passes through its leaves and the inside voice that comes from within the tree. It's the voice of the wood itself."

"My father says that each tree is different from the next. Every piece of wood even," replied Mike.

But he couldn't hear the voice. He listened intently but all he could hear was the sound of his own heartbeat.

THE NEXT DAY Mike was back on the square. There wasn't a cop in sight so he went to the cellar and got the three large pieces of linoleum that he'd stored there. He tore the carpet into smaller pieces, which he tossed out into the traffic. The carpet swept through the warm air and twisted like drunken birds amid the hurrying trucks and cars. Brakes screeched, horns honked as the ragged missiles swooped in front of windshields or bounced off hoods. Mike hid behind Kleinberg's truck piled high with laundry. Drivers cursed and swore and looked confusedly around for the perpetrator, their heads bobbing from side to side like the heads of wooden puppets. Mike was giddy with enjoyment. He had never felt such power and glory before. He smiled broadly and General Grant smiled back from his noble bronze horse. They both understood what it meant to surprise one's enemies and see them scatter in confusion. For the first time since he'd come to the square, the general had taken his keen eyes from the horizon and turned them toward a living human being. He hadn't even done that the day that Deucey had hit the great home run. Mike let sail another linoleum bird but as this triumphant eagle spread its wings over a Chevy coupe the cop of the fiery head, Officer O'Ruarke, appeared at the corner.

"You again!" shouted the cop as the Chevy braked loudly. He came charging down the block, a mountain of blue with two glittering silver shields. Mike dropped the rest of the carpeting and headed for Forest Place. But O'Ruarke of the fiery head gained on him with his long legs and huge black shoes just as the Smiling Clown gained on Tiny in her dream. When Mike saw the cop's shadow overtaking him, he realized he'd never make the corner on the straightaway without the cop grabbing him, so he stopped short all of a sudden and dodged behind a parked car.

O'Ruarke stumbled as he tried to change direction.

Mike headed up the square toward Brevoort. He was planning to run down the cellar and out the back door into the yards where it would be easier to lose the flatfoot by climbing a few fences. But O'Ruarke was gaining on him again and as Mike neared the corner two women with baby carriages came round it, blocking the way. Mike could have got through only by pushing past the women and he didn't want to upset the carriages with the babies in them so he stopped dead in his tracks and let the flatfoot grab him. But O'Ruarke tripped as he stopped short and fell to the ground.

The women laughed at the cop's clumsiness and Mike knew that the fiery-head policeman would kill him now if he got his hands on him.

Down the square with him again with the cop after him and he got this idea that he'd hide up on top of the laundry truck amid the bundles of wash. He climbed on the ladder on the back of the truck and was about halfway up when O'Ruarke got hold of his legs and pulled him down into the gutter.

"You little bastard!" said O'Ruarke as he put one of his big black-shoed feet on Mike's back while he took out his manacles and handcuffed Mike.

It had all been a big game for Mike until the moment he felt the steel of the cuffs on his wrists. The adventure vanished then as the cop tightened the screws. For the first time in his life, he couldn't move his hands or stretch his arms where he wanted. The most basic freedom, the freedom of his limbs, was being denied him. He might as well be in an iron lung, have polio, be crippled. His heart began to pound and he lost his breath as the tears welled up like sea water out of his eyes.

The cop picked him up by the scruff of his neck.

"Little punk," he said angrily. "Snot nose."

"Isn't he a little young for handcuffs?" asked one of the baby-carriage women.

"They're never too young," replied O'Ruarke.

The policeman got his name and address out of Mike and took him around to 931 where he lived. The cop pushed his bell but there was no answer. His mother wasn't home.

"Typical!" snarled the cop. "You're out running around like the Wild Man of Borneo and she ain't even home!"

Mike said she was probably shopping, feeling he had to defend his mother from the tone of the cop's remark. O'Ruarke chained Mike to the front fence and told him they'd wait for her.

It wasn't long till Mike saw her coming up Brevoort from the Avenue. She had her arms full of groceries in brown paper bags but she walked sprightly with her dark hair bouncing on her shoulders like the fair maidens in his father's songs. He knew she hadn't seen him and the cop yet. He dreaded the moment she would. God knew what she'd do! He wished she'd remain forever coming up the sidewalk like one of those eternal *cailíns*.

The moment she saw them a shock went through her body and she lost the ease of her flesh. Up the last bit of sidewalk with her, hurrying, and struggling with the paper bags.

"What did he do, Sarjint," she asked excitedly, "that you have him under lock like that?"

A bag slipped from her arms as she spoke and scattered carrots and Brussels sprouts over the blue slate sidewalk. Annie paid them no heed but listened to O'Ruarke as he recounted the events of the past two days. As the policeman spoke she cast hard glances at Mike, who lowered his eyes, looking at his feet through his chained wrists. Never had he felt so low.

The cop lectured his mother on how to bring up kids and she smiled and shook her head at everything he said but it was only when the tears came to her eyes and she got down on her knees to gather up the vegetables that O'Ruarke unchained him.

"A thousand thanks to you, Sarjint, that you didn't arrest him," she said, down on her knees amid the yellow carrots and green sprouts. She looked over at Mike.

"*Mo léan géar gur thug tú náire domh os comhair an tsaoil, a spailpín!*" she screeched. "Disgracing me in front of the neighbors! Don't be standing there with long arms. Help me gather these up before they *be's* trampled on."

Never had vegetables felt so hard and cold as these sprouts and carrots to Mike.

"I've never been so humiliated in me life as I am now and it's you have done it," she hissed at him.

Mike felt like he would burst out crying but he held the tears back because he didn't want to give O'Ruarke the satisfaction of seeing him bawl again.

"If we don't teach our children discipline," said O'Ruarke towering over them, "the whole country's gonna go to pot. The whites are becoming as bad as the niggers. Soon it'll be the law of the jungle."

With that he walked off.

That evening when his father got home from work he gave Mike a slap when he heard what had happened. All during dinner his parents criticized him while Eamonn and Peggy smirked. Eamonn told him that he should say a rosary to make up for what he'd done until he got a chance to go to confession the next Saturday.

"Pray!" Eamonn said. "Pray the rosary."

According to his brother, there was no doubt that Mike had committed a mortal sin by his willful disobedience to the authority of Officer O'Ruarke—for according to Catholic doctrine, policemen, like teachers and parents, were the lawful representatives of God on Earth and had to be obeyed. Mike had committed a mortal sin and therefore had merited eternal damnation.

Later as he lay on his bed in the dark with the red glow of the Joy Restaurant's neon sign reflecting on the ceiling, it was easy to imagine the reality of hellfire and damnation. He was sure he could feel the world turning through empty black space with no "up" or "down" or "East" or "West," abandoned by God like the girl in *Dónal Óg*, and himself slipping off the surface of the globe because he no longer had the gravity boots of Sanctifying Grace to hold him on. Sin had destroyed the Sanctifying Grace that had filled his soul and shielded it from the terrible wrath of a God who could carry him off into eternal darkness far from the familiar breathing of his sleeping sister and brother. A God who had slaughtered the firstborn babes of the Egyptians, who would loose plagues and earthquakes on mankind as quick as he'd turn his starry fist; a God who had let the A-bomb get made and who people said would appear in the great mushroom cloud at the end of the world.

Eamonn had told him to pray, so he crawled off the bed and got on his knees, the linoleum feeling lukewarm and sticky beneath them. He tried to pray but the words wouldn't come. His mouth dried every time he began to recite the rosary. He kept hearing Eamonn's voice telling him to pray and the more he heard it the less he could even think of the words of any prayer though he knew twenty prayers off by heart.

He felt hot inside as if Mount Vesuvius was boiling up inside him instead of beside Naples where Mrs. Collucci's people were. Indeed, he felt like the mountain, as if his flesh had become soil and stone and a great fire within.

He leapt from the floor and put on his clothes and sneakers. Out the window and down the fire escape he went, to the street below. He began to run. He didn't know where, he just ran. He ran through the square and past Grant guarding the dark horizon, down Forest Place, full of black leaves and black sky.

When he stopped running he was in front of Empire Hall. He climbed up the fire escape in the alley. Six floors up, undetected, past bright and dark windows until he reached Tiny's apartment. There was a light in the living room and he could see Mrs. Evans with her yellow curls dozing in front of the television set. His parents couldn't afford a TV set. The bedroom was dark and he climbed in the window.

"Tiny!" he whispered. "Tiny."

There was no answer. He could see the closet in the light that streamed in under the door. He opened it and felt around in the dark until he found the picture of the Smiling Clown. It wasn't very large so he had no trouble getting it out the window and down the fire escape. He had to drop it from the first-floor fire escape, and when he climbed down after it he tumbled a garbage can.

"What's goin' on out there?" someone yelled, but by the that time he was up the block already, the picture wedged under his arm.

He looked at the clown in the faint yellow light of the lamp-post. The smile was evil just like Tiny had said.

He turned the face away from him and took the picture down into the cellar, feeling his way through the pitch blackness until he reached the back room where he hid it in a drawer of the dresser that his father was saving. The dresser that stood in front of where Deucey hid his pistol.

When he closed the drawer on the clown, he felt good. He hadn't decided what he would do with him. He'd ask Tiny what to do. Then again, he thought, maybe it would be better not to tell her that he'd lifted it at all.

Maybe he'd sell it to the junk man who came along Brevoort every Tuesday with his horse and wagon. He bought everything.

Maybe he'd sell it to Tommy the Hat himself. Maybe it had real value. Tommy would know. Maybe he could get like five bucks for it.

Maybe he'd keep it for a while until he'd made up his mind. He wasn't exactly sure why he had taken it in the first place. He hadn't thought about it beforehand. He'd just done it. In any event, now that he had the Smiling Clown, he didn't know what he'd do with it.

He climbed up the fire escape again but instead of going into his house he continued on to the roof. He looked up at the stars.

The stars could be seen from the roof unlike from the street where the glare of the lampposts obscured them. There above he could see the Plough crooked across the sky; and there was the *Bodach* and his *buaile* where he milked his cows. It was by the stars that the Driscolls had sailed the seas in the olden times his father had told him. They had no compasses, no radar, just these shining stars and constellations. He stared into space and he could feel the Earth turning under his feet but it didn't frighten him this time. He didn't feel like he was going to slip off the edge of the world. He felt protected as if the stars would guide him to a safe harbor just as they had guided his ancestors.

TWO WEEKS LATER on Sunday afternoon, there was a stick-ball game. It was a memorable game not because of another long homer but because of a fight, a fight that started when one of the members of the Bedford Christian Church tried to pull his car out into the street while the game was in progress.

There was one down in the home third inning with Tommy the Hat at bat when the colored man got into his car. Donny Muldoon, the Brevoort giant, went and stood in front of the car with his hands up and told the colored guy not to move the car. Mike was watching from across the way, from his lookout at the base of statue, near the hat with the money in it. The next thing he saw was the car jump out into the street knocking Donny out of the way. As it turned out later the colored man thought Donny was trying to start trouble or rob him or something like that so he hit the accelerator. In any event, Donny went down and the car took off down the square with Deucey, Bunny and a couple of other Brevoort Boys in pursuit. It turned onto Forest Place and disappeared from view.

Donny wasn't hurt bad and the car hadn't run over him but he was mad and he went into the old RKO Grant, with its marquee now saying WE PREACH CHRIST CRUCIFIED, and he was shouting, "I'm gonna break some nigger's face for this!"

Those were his exact words, which Mike heard clearly because he'd crossed the street and followed Donny. Deucey and Bunny went right in after Donny shaking their fists. All the big guys crowded under the marquee and Mike was pushed back so he had to get on the hood of a car to see what was going on. It was a '38 De Soto belonging to Mr. Collucci. Mike was just in time to see Donny and Deucey and Bunny Imp getting pushed out the beautiful brass front doors by a dozen or so colored men dressed up in long black robes. One of the men was wearing a robe bordered with purple; he looked like the chief minister to Mike.

It seemed like the ruckus might be ended because the pushing and shoving had stopped for a moment. But then Deucey punched one of the black guys in the mouth, knocking him off his feet.

Then the minister called Deucey a "bastard."

When Deucey heard those words, his hair seemed to thicken and stand on end and his face became contorted with rage. To Mike it looked like one of his eyes doubled in size so that he thought that it would burst out of its socket while the other shrank to the size of a burning black coal. His body became like a cat's, the ribs moving apart as he crouched and then sprang onto the minister, punching him in the face and tearing at him like a wild beast. Mike saw blood shoot out of the clergyman's nose. Then it was a free-for-all with the colored churchmen and the Brevoort Boys pounding at each other with their fists.

That was how the Brevoort Race Riot started and it didn't end until the cops showed up ten minutes later. They waded in with their nightsticks banging guys over the head and, later, people said the cops sent more guys to the hospital than the original fight. In any event by the time the battle was over there were a lot of broken noses and black eyes. The glass in the beautiful brass doors was all smashed and so was the windshield of the minister's car.

"No nigger'll ever call Deucey Doyle a bastard again," was how Bunny Imp summarized the day's action.

Neither Deucey nor Donny Muldoon nor any other of the Brevoort Boys were arrested that day but two of the colored men were, for assaulting a policeman. The charges were dropped later. From then on, Sundays, there was a cop stationed in front of the old RKO Grant during the stickball season to prevent any more trouble between the races.

Mike had never seen blood spilt like he saw that Sunday from his perch on the hood of Mr. Collucci's De Soto. The sound of noses being broken, and skulls being pounded on the sidewalk made him feel sick inside but he'd persevered and didn't give in to the urge to run away and throw up. This, indeed, was the greatest summer of his life, he thought. He had seen Deucey's homer and now the battle of the RKO. Of all the things he'd seen, he knew it would be Deucey's anger that he'd never be able to forget.

A MAY MORNING AND Jimmy was telling Mike that he should go to Brooklyn Tech and study engineering.

"I wanna be a carpenter like you, Daddy," Mike replied.

"Och, the world is going against carpenters and joiners. It's going against craftsmen of every sorts, *a Mhicilín*. There's no weavers anymore. No fullers. There's no coopers. No smiths. Shoemakers don't be making shoes anymore and tailors don't be making clothes. Soon the only people who'll know anything at all will be the boyos with the university diplomas. Nobody will have a head on their shoulders but those fellas. If I was your age I'd go with the engineering, the architecture. That's where the future is and they're honorable trades."

He paused and looked out the open window at the buildings cross the way.

"You know, this whole city was inside someone's head one time." He tapped himself on the temple with his index finger. "All these buildings, all these streets, all the tunnels, all the subway trains, all the aeroplanes was once inside some fella's skull. It's all in there and if you're an engineer you'll get a chance to let it out, you will. So study and do good in school, *a mhic-ó*. Jesus! won't I be grand in me old age. You'll build your mammy and me a big house in the country and Eamonn will be the Bishop of Brooklyn and he'll shake the holy water on it."

"Eamonn's gonna be Pope by that time, he says," added Mike.

"Ah, he's clever enough for the job and he's got the toes for it according to Mrs. Collucci," Jimmy giggled.

"Don't you believe in the toes?" Mike asked hopefully.

"Well, sure I wouldn't want to be contradicting your mother and Mrs. Collucci, but I've never seen a picture of the Pope's toes at all. He's forever wearing shoes in the photos I see. Don't be tellin' your brother Eamonn what I'm sayin' as he lays great store by his toes now, but if the Pope had special toes, sure he'd be showin' them off, don't you think? If Eamonn's to be the Pope, it won't be on account of his toes at all, at all."

"Eamonn says they've got lots of secret things in the Vatican that they don't tell anyone about. They've got the True Cross there and nobody sees it except the monk who cuts the little slivers off it that they put in altars. And they've got the letter from Our Lady of Fatima about the End of the World. Nobody sees that but the Pope himself."

"Oh, I don't know at all," said Jimmy, getting up to clear the table. He put the dishes in the sink and everything away but the butter, which he left out so it would be soft for Annie when she got up to eat. Butter is balm for the heart, the ould ones used say.

Mike watched him put on his work boots.

He kissed Mike good-bye and put his lunchpail under his arm. Then it was out the door with him and down the stairs.

Mike felt left behind and lonely as he did every morning when he heard those footsteps echoing in the hallway, fearing it would be the last he'd hear of his father, that the world would swallow him up. He hurried to the bedroom window past the sleeping forms of his brother and sister. He looked down at Brevoort Street through the rusty black bars of the fire escape and felt like a prisoner, cut off from the world of men.

He watched Jimmy as he hurried across the cobblestoned street to the trolley stop. Other men were waiting there. Like his father they wore short jackets mostly and carried black metal lunchpails tucked under their arms. They stood with their hands in their pockets, smoking. The cigarettes bobbed up and down in their mouths as they talked but never fell from their lips. They could even laugh without losing them. The trolley car came and halted. It blocked his view of Jimmy and the others. Then it began to pull away with an electric whine. For a instant Mike hoped that his father would still be there after the trolley left, he and the other men laughing and talking, joking and gesturing in a halo of cigarette smoke. But he wasn't and of course Mike knew he wouldn't be. All that was left of him was a cigarette smoking in the gutter next to the track that glistened silver in the early sun.

He was about to turn away from the window when he saw the great Deucey Doyle coming out of the alleyway that ran behind the former RKO Grant, now the Bedford Christian Church.

He'd never seen Deucey up so early in his entire life. The earliest he'd ever seen him was at lunchtime. Deucey used to hang out late at night. Charlie said his uncle hung with the crowd in the Bedford Rest bar until two or three in the morning.

Deucey was standing at the mouth of the alley looking around a bit nervously it seemed to Mike. Then Bunny Imperatore came out the alley and both of them walked off together down the block and disappeared into Santo's Bakery.

Mike figured there must be something important going on, so he put on his clothes and the hat with the brush in its band that he always wore when he was doing any kind of detective work. He took the dog, Sparks, with him because if you had a dog you could stand as long as you wanted almost anywhere without attracting attention.

There was no one in front of Santo's when he got there. There was no one at the counter and as usual the shelves were empty and covered with white paper. Of course Mike realized he couldn't know what the Deuce and the Imp were doing inside in the backroom but the idea that he was nearby, that he was in proximity while something significant was going on, made him feel important and "with it."

He lit a cigarette that he'd lifted from his father's pack and tried to keep it between his lips without screwing his face up too much. There was a certain amount of squint that gave you a look of hardness around the eyes, that seemed to mean that you knew what you were doing. All the tough guys who hung around Santo's had it.

The dog pulled him farther out into the gutter so he had to switch the cigarette to his fingers to keep from losing it. She was making pee, a swift yellow river that cascaded through the cobblestones like the Colorado, seen from ten thousand feet up through the bombsight of a B-29, running through the Grand Canyon, pictured in his geography book. The length of the Paraná and the products of Paraguay he knew by heart. Sparks looked like some animal saint when she was peeing because her eyes would get all lit up like she was seeing God just like in the picture over the side altar in the parish church. It was called *The Apotheosis of Saint John the Evangelist* and it had the saint meeting God as he was dying. He had that look of transformation on his face that Lon Chaney, Jr. used to get when he was looking up at the full moon right before he'd turn into the Wolf Man. Tiny had that look too the time she had him hugging the tree on Forest Place just before she closed her eyes. Brother Barometer used to get it sometimes when he talked about how wonderful it must have been to have been thrown to the lions in ancient Rome or to have your heart ripped out by the Mohawks while you were still alive, like happened to St. Isaac Jogues and Jean de Brébeuf, the North American Martyrs who had their shrine way upstate at Auriesville. Vinnie Collucci had seen the place because Mr. Collucci had a car. He'd seen the Baseball Hall of Fame at Cooperstown and the Ausable Chasm and the Howe Caverns and he never let anybody forget it. Mike figured if Jimmy went to work in the Navy Yard, they'd be able to get a car and see everything upstate too. Mr. Collucci took them to LaGuardia Airport one time the year before to see the planes landing and taking off. He used to go out there a lot. He kept pigeons. Mrs. Collucci complained he loved the pigeons more than anything in the world. He was in love with flight, she'd said.

Sparks finished her pee and kicked her feet out behind her. She danced around in delight with her eyes sparkling. That's how she'd got her name, from the sparks in her eyes.

Deucey and Bunny came out of Santo's with Tommy the Hat. They walked past Mike like he wasn't there and went into the

Joy Restaurant. Mike watched them get a booth. He went in and sat in a booth next to theirs. He sat with his back to them and made like he was looking out the window. Martha, the waitress, came over and tickled him under the chin.

"What can I do for you, Michael?" she asked, smiling, with her sing-song Swedish accent. "Look at those big blue eyes, a charmboat just like your father."

Mike turned as red as one of the tomatoes that was ripening in the window. He wanted to crawl under the table. He ordered a glass of milk and a chocolate donut.

He gave a quick glance over his shoulder to see if Deucey and the others were looking at him. They weren't. For once in his life he was thanking God that big guys didn't pay attention to little guys like him. They were talking intensely. Maybe they were planning a job, he thought. A burglary. Maybe they were gonna burglarize the colored church.

People said that Willie the Actor Sutton, the greatest thief of all, had planned his first jobs right here in the Joy when he was around Deucey's age. Willie was the most popular crook since Dillinger. Back in the Depression everybody loved Dillinger, according to his father. There'd been a national petition to pardon him and Jimmy had signed it. But the G-men killed him anyway in spite of the millions of signatures.

The Lady in Red fingered him. That was the lowest thing you could do. Sing. Squeal on a guy.

The same thing had happened to Willie. He was out washing his car when Schuster saw him and squealed on him. That's how the cops pinched him. In front of his house washing his car.

Willie never hurt nobody, like Dillinger. There was no harm in robbing banks, people said.

The worse thing you could do was be a squealer. That's why the mob had Schuster killed. A lesson to all potential squealers. Back in Ireland, they used to shoot informers. Or tar and feather them. There was nothing lower than a stool pigeon.

"Four cases," said Tommy the Hat. "Are youse sure the shit is safe up there on the roof?"

"No sweat," said Deucey. "We had tons of shit on the *Franklin*. Shit never blew even when we got hit and were on fire."

"The Deuce used to arm bombs," said Bunny. "He knows all about the shit. Ba-boom! Ba-bomb!"

"Keep it down," said the Hat. "Act your age, Bun."

"It'd have to get hit by lightning to go off," said Deucey with authority. "Lightning."

"We brung it all the way from Jersey in the back of a car and nuttin' happened to us," said Bunny.

"I can see that," said the Hat, vaguely sarcastic. "As far as gettin' rid of the stuff, I'll have to talk wit' some people. It ain't exactly hot watches we're tryin' to fence here. People ain't gonna buy this offa you out the back of a car. It's what they call a 'special market' item."

"People use the stuff for all kinds of construction," objected Bunny.

"Yeah, but I gotta fin' out who, and who would wanna take some offa my hands. Get me?"

"Got you," said Deucey.

"You got four boxes, right?"

"But we're only sellin' three," said Deucey.

"What you gonna do with the other one?"

Deucey leaned forward over the table toward The Hat and smiled.

"We're gonna blow the nigger church," he whispered.

"The RKO, you mean?" asked The Hat in disbelief.

"Affirmative," replied Deucey, switching to military talk.

"You gotta be kiddin' me," said Tommy the Hat.

"We ain't kiddin'," said Bunny Imp. "Ba-Boom!"

"Youse guys is outta your tree!"

"We wan' 'em out of Precious Blood," said Deucey.

"Yeah, we don' wan' 'em ruining the neighborhood like they ruined downtown," said Bunny.

"Hey, don't get me wrong. I ain't no nigger-lover and I wan' 'em to go back where they come from too, but blowin' up the RKO, guys, that ain't the way to do it."

"Nobody calls the Deuce a 'crazy bastid' and gets away wit' it," said Bunny. "We gonna teach that jig minister a lesson he ain't ever gonna forget."

"Bastard? You gonna blow the place up 'cause he called you a bastard?" Tommy laughed. "You ain't never been called a bastard before? Mother o' God, what wouldya do if the guy called you a cocksucker? Blow up Harlem?"

Deucey reached across the table and grabbed Tommy the Hat by the lapels of his coat.

"Lissen, Hat," he whispered, his voice hissing with rage, "a 'cocksucker' is one thing but a 'bastard'—nobody but nobody calls me a 'bastard'!"

112

"All right, Deucey," said The Hat, fearful and apologetic. "I get you. You don't like the word. You got evvy right not to."

"What do you mean, I got evvy right? Whaddaya mean by dat?" replied Deucey, squeezing the lapels between his clenched fists. "You tryin'a say I am what that coon called me? You tryin'a say that?"

"No way Deucey, no way," replied Tommy the Hat. "You ain't no bastard. You ain't."

"Okay then, but watch your mouth from here on out," said Deucey, releasing his grip on Tommy's coat.

"Sorry, Deucey," he said as he smoothed out the wrinkles.

For a minute the three just sat there sipping at their coffee and looking at each other until Bunny said, "Do we got a deal, Tommyboy? You fence the three boxes for us?"

"I dunno," said Tommy the Hat. "I mean if youse guys gave me all the dynamite I probably could fence it for you. Whatever it's worth, I got no idea right now. But if youse actually is gonna do the RKO thing, evvy flatfoot in Brooklyn'll be out scratchin' around to see who done it and they hear I handled three boxes of the shit? You gotta be kiddin' me. I'll be in the can quicker than you can turn your fist. With all due respect to your feelings, Deuce, I can only do the deal if you don't do no bombing."

The last word he whispered.

"We can sell the stuff on our own," replied Deucey defiantly.

"Yeah, we don' need you," added Bunny.

"Maybe you're right, but if you wanna talk more about it, you know where you can reach me. Why don't you think about it a couple of days?" said The Hat, conciliatory. "You said you got enough of the shit to blow up the neighborhood? Are you really sure it's safe up there? And what about the block? I mean like how you gonna blow up these niggers without blowing evvybody else up. Your brother and his kids, they live on Brevoort. What about them? What about the boys at Santo's? People are gonna get killed."

"Nobody's gonna get killed," said Deucey. "Even the niggers. I don't hate niggers. I just don' wan' 'em in Precious Blood. We're gonna do it in the middle of the night like we was doing a warehouse job. . . ."

"Except instead of boosting furs we're gonna be boosting some fuckin' walls," added Bunny, giggling.

"Right, Bun Babe. Nobody's gonna be inside and nobody's gonna be around. Nobody gets hurt. But the niggers, the niggers don't come back!"

"I got business, guys," said The Hat getting up, dropping six bits on the table to cover the check. "You wanna talk to me tonight I'll be over Santo's till Santa Anita and Hollywood Park are in."

They watched Tommy leave.

"All his money goes on the horses," said Deucey with contempt.

"Maybe he's right though, Deucey. Maybe we could forget the niggers for a while. We could make a nice bit of bread outta the stuff. Go to the track ourselves. Pick up some broads."

"Ah, he's a worm," replied Deucey. "Got no balls. That's why he's a fence. Afraid to boost shit himself but he'll make money on us doing it. Worm."

Deucey and Bunny left soon after. They split up on the

corner and Mike followed Deucey till he saw him go into the building where he lived above the Bedford Rest beergarden.

Mike was scared and elated. Scared that the "stuff" would explode and elated that he was "in" on a big deal.

If you wanted to find out who was who and what was what in the world, Mike was convinced that you could do it a lot quicker by following guys like the Deuce and The Hat around than by reading any schoolbook or even one of those big thick library books that Eamonn always had his nose stuck in.

He stopped at Benny's candy store to buy his mother the morning paper with his last three cents. He'd spent three days' candy money on his milk and donut including the nickel tip he'd left for Martha the waitress. He would have to deliver some prescriptions for Mr. Kaufman at the drug store to make some money. Bill Doyle was at the counter drinking Bromo-Seltzer. Mike greeted him and Bill nodded. He drank the bromo down like he was drinking poison, then he gave out a large belch.

"AAAAAHHHH! JEEEEEZZZZZ! That's the stuff!" he said.

Mike wondered why anyone would drink stuff like that for breakfast. He must be late for work too, Mike thought.

There were other men in Benny's drinking plain seltzer for two cents and they were getting the daily line of horses and making notes with stubby pencils, the kind his father used when he was writing measurements down on the backs of envelopes. It seemed like his father never used looseleaf or real paper, it was always envelopes or paper bags or matchbooks he would write things on. There didn't seem to be any blank paper or pencil sharpeners in the world of men.

His father never bet the horses or the numbers and he never went into Santo's Bakery for anything outside of buying an ice in the summer. He never did anything illegal except buying the Irish Sweepstakes, and firecrackers and Roman candles for the Fourth of July. Maybe the only thing he ever stole in his life was that coffin lid back home. And was it really possible to steal from your own father?

For a moment the vision of his father floating off on the green water made his heart stop. He hoped that his mother's nightmares couldn't pursue her across the waves, that they were only powerful in Erin. That was the way it was with the *síoganna*. They never crossed the ocean with the immigrants, bound forever to their hills and rocky places. He hoped her dream of the Handsome Man would stay home, too, in the dark streetless nights of the glen.

His father didn't do anything illegal; all he did was work and talk to people, to everybody including Swedish waitresses. Work and talk. Tell stories and sing. He loved to sing on Sunday afternoons and at big nights and weddings and bazaars and even at the Italian feast down on Grand Avenue.

His father was always embarrassing him in public the way Michael saw it. Mike didn't like the attention. He wanted his father to be quiet in public. It would have been different had they been back home among their own kind, great talkers and singers were respected there. But not in New York. No time for talk, no time for song. You had to be tough here. Like Deucey.

.   .   .

116

ANNIE WAS UP at seven and had the oatmeal cooking for the children's breakfast. *Brachán.* Eamonn and Peggy were still in bed but Mike and Sparks were gone. Mike was out exploring no doubt. She looked out the window. The sunlight bounced blinding off the windows across the street; the shadows thrown by the stoops and lintels of the doorways and windows looked painted and the alley behind the old RKO impenetrably black. To think it was a colored church and only twenty years before, Frank Evans and Eileen was dancing away in it, back in the age of the silent movies. The world changes.

Mike was nowhere to be seen. She had never encountered as curious a boy since her brother Manus at home. Sometimes she'd think of him as Manus and call him Manus absentmindedly. It was a great pity the boy didn't have fields to run in and rocks to climb, bowls of Dé Danaan's butter to be digging out of the boggy places, the butter long since turned to fine gold dust. It was a pity that he'd only these streets to wander in but that's where the work was and where the Irish were.

Jimmy had gotten the offer of a job upstate a few years before; they'd decided against it as neither one of them could imagine being that far away from the sound of Irish voices. She took the tip of a finger full of butter and stuck it in her mouth. Good. But there was no butter to compare with the butter her own mother churned at home. The best butter in all the glen and she was always got a good price for it. Ach, but selling the butter was more important to her mother than she herself had been.

She remembered getting up well before daybreak when she was only a wee *cutach* to help her mother feed the beasts. They used to heat up a large tub of water and while the water was coming to a boil they'd be cutting up the turnips. They'd pour the hot water on them to soften them up. Sure her mother didn't want the beasts turning up their huge noses at cold turnips.

It was only after the cattle had got their mess that she could eat her bit. *Brachán* it was, left over from the supper the night before. Sometimes it'd be cold, for her mother worried little about her turning her nose up at food whatever shape it was in. She wouldn't be getting her dinner till she returned from school in the afternoon and nothing between but a cold *préataí* or two, or an oaten *bonnach* she'd be taking with her.

In the dark guts of winter it was she who'd be out breaking the ice on the trough so the animals could drink while the men of the house including her brother Manus used still be in their beds. It seemed to her that a girl like herself had a childhood that was three years shorter than a *gasúr*'s like Manus. Oh, boys had the sweet life, full of pretending and sport and the only time the men called them out in earnest when they were wee was to watch the bull going at the cow or the horse coupling with the mare.

Oh, it was all great fun and games making certain the horse got his horn in the right spot. Sure the men would have a two-year-old *gasúr* out with them looking at the action but devil a woman they'd want watching. As if women knew nothing about such things! Just who did they think was having the babies for them? The *síoganna?*

Och, men. They always had *that* on their minds, no matter, as if it was something new and wonderful they had between their legs.

Och, these Irish-American men were terrible altogether. They looked at you like they owned you, not a bit of shyness to them like the country men at home.

Oh, the narrowbacks was terrible. The women the worst. Chewing gum and smoking cigarettes and standing by their strollers outside Bauer's ice-cream parlor, jabbering away, when they should be home cleaning, cooking, putting themselves to good use.

Och, and that Deucey Doyle and his crowd mooching about with long arms empty, a big strong *scafaire,* every mother's son of them, who ought be out being useful, working hard even if it was digging a ditch or carrying a hod to the eyes of the world, for there was nothing dishonorable in work and it was by the sweat of your brow that you lived in this life. But it was only one sort of work that crowd had their eye on. Jesus, you felt like you were naked entirely going past them fellows.

Deucey Doyle and Bunny Imperatore. Nobody even knew what their Christian names were except their mothers. Thanks be to God Mrs. Doyle died before seeing her son turn out like he did. Poor Mrs. Imperatore. Irish and Italians. Sure you wouldn't find a crowd of Protestants or Presbyterians mooching around like that. They'd be doing something useful with themselves.

That's why they live in big houses, home. All over the world Catholics live in little cabins on the side of mountains, making babies just like the Orangemen said. Och, the Gaels have that in them, despite the priests preaching against it. Tailors always had the name for being like that. Traveling from house to house there was many a woman that had to fight them off. Maybe the

Doyles had tailor blood in them. The way that Deucey looks at you, flexing those big muscles of his.

And Michael worships the ground he walks on. Mother of mercy, what would she do if Mike turned out like him. What women have to bear in this life! She'd have to ask Nancy about the Doyles' blood. Not that Nancy would tell her even though they'd know each other since they were *cailíns* in national school. Odd bird, and secretive, even after all these years!

She even wondered about her Jimmy. The Handsome Man, always talking with the women. There wasn't a woman on Brevoort Street he hadn't passed the time of day with. And the way that Eileen Evans looked at him sometimes, she was never sure that something wasn't going on between them. She wondered.

What would she do if there was? Out with him, she could never live with a man who'd done that to her. Their marriage would be over.

MIKE HANDED HIS mother the newspaper when he came in the door.

"Out galavantin' again?" she asked, smiling.

"Took Sparks for a long walk."

"Where's it you go?"

"Nowhere."

He could hear Eamonn saying his prayers in the bedroom. Peggy was running the water in the bathroom. She was staring at herself in the mirror. He used to peek through the keyhole at her sometimes. She could look at herself for hours.

Annie put a bowl of *brachán* on the table. Hot milk, butter and brown sugar on it.

He sat and looked at it.

"Eat," she said encouragingly. "There's strength in that for studying."

He took a mouthful or two of the oatmeal then began to pick at it.

"Eating those donuts again when you were out?" she said, glancing up from her tea.

"Not me," he replied, trying to look innocent.

"Is it sick you are then?"

"Not hungry. That's all."

"Och, you'd better be hungry when you're young or you'll never be hungry when you're old," she said, with a note of concern in her voice.

She was thinking of Wee Kitty, her sister. The loss of appetite was the first thing that happened in her case and it wasn't long after that she got sick and then she was gone like foam from the river. A short life she got and looked like an wee angel there in the *corp house* with her fair curls and the white sheets around her.

Mike wasn't lying this time. He wasn't hungry and he knew it wasn't the donut or the slice of rye bread he'd had earlier that was taking away his appetite. It was the shock of what he had overheard in the Joy Restaurant that was the cause of it. The *stuff.* He was finally realizing that it was for real and not something made up he'd heard on the radio or seen in the movies. Real. But the idea that four boxes of dynamite were indeed sitting on the roof of the RKO Grant or the Bedford Christian Church was incredible. Maybe he had dreamt it. Maybe it was the blood of the Shiels coming out in him, people of powerful dreams, of signs, warnings and premonitions.

"Where was I, Mammy, when you got up this morning?" he asked.

"That's what I'm after asking you, *a Mhicilín*. Or is it a guessing game we're playing?" She smiled.

"I was out, wasn't I? I wasn't sleepin', was I?"

"You were out, indeed. Can't you remember that?" She looked concerned at him. "Are you alright?"

"Oh, it's nothin'," he replied, shaking his head and taking another mouthful of the *brachán*.

"C'mon," she said, "what's on you?"

"Why do the white people hate the colored people so much here?"

"Mother of God, why are you thinkin' about such things so early on a beautiful morning like this one?"

"Heard people talking," he replied.

"Well, all I know is they say the very same things about the colored people here as they did about us at home. That we were all lazy and good for nothing but making babies and drinking and fighting. Och, I tell you there's little difference between the Orangemen at home and Ku Klux Klan here except that one wears sashes instead of sheets."

Annie sat back in her rocking and thought for a moment before continuing.

"Did I ever tell you the story about when I was young and going the road to the national school at Ardán Donn? Well I was late as usual as I had many chores to do and I knew that *scalladóir* of a woman, Mistress MacGillheany, would be ready and waiting to flay me with that sally rod of hers, for she brooked no lateness for any reason even if she knew it was the parents keeping the *childer* late. It's only since I came here that I found out what she was. She was what they call a sadist. Cruel and liking it.

"Well, there was a landlord the name of Captain Cadgette and he was the head Orangeman in the glen—scorch his head— and he was terrible against the Gaels, as we were all *Papishes*, as they called us. He lived in a big house like landlords did and it was surrounded by tall old trees. You couldn't see it even if you was up on the height of the Cloigeann looking down. Well, he was a fanatic against us and he wouldn't let a true-blooded Irishman step on his land for fear he'd catch the contagion of Popery or the like. Sure he wouldn't even buy a strange egg, it might have been laid by a Catholic hen! He wouldn't hire Catholics as servants or ploughmen and he gave these posts to the poorest *Sasanachs* of the glen, people like the Wilsons from Rúscaí.

"Now Bella Wilson was friendly with us Shiels and she used call in when she was passing by. She was working as a kitchen maid for Cadgette and she'd be telling my mother about his antics. Cursing the Pope of Rome every Sunday with a glass of sherry before he ate and toasting King William of Orange like he was still breathing and riding that white horse of his. Bella said that the last thing every Cadgette did on his deathbed was to curse the Pope, for the curse of dying man is the worst as it can never be gone back on. Well, I was young and impressionable and I was terrified of this Captain Cadgette and when I got to the place in the road where it went through his land I used always direct my feet to the middle of the road lest I step on a sod of his land—sure I thought I'd die if I touched it.

"Now it was the time of the Troubles and I'm hurrying along down the middle of the road so I don't touch the Captain's land at all. *Mhuise* what do I hear but a lorry coming behind me and I think it's Niall Mac Dónaill from Gort Rua, for his was the only lorry in that side of the country in those days. I'm worrying about the Captain and minding my feet so they don't wander off the road. Well, the lorry is getting louder as it comes down around the bend by Más na Ríona and it doesn't sound like Niall's lorry to me anymore, so I turn round and look and what did I see but a big enormous Crossley Tender full of Black and Tans bearing down on me. There was big ugly gun on it, a machine gun I think they call them now.

"Well, what was to be done? Och, I was 'twixt the fires of *Bealtaine*, I was, for I couldn't stay on the road and I couldn't get off it for fear I'd die if I touched Captain Cadgette's land. Sure I was still of a foolish age. *M'anam,* the lorry was on the point of swallowing me up under its wheels and I was frozen to the spot with panic.

"Well, I was sure I was dead when at the very last moment I felt a hand pull me off to the side. And do you know it was me sister's hand, the hand of Wee Kitty who'd been three years dead at the time. Sure, I thought I saw her face, too, as the lorry rushed by full to the edges with Black and Tans and their guns.

The force of it knocked me over, the wind, you know. You see it was her spirit keeping me from harm.

"Things like that happen at home every day and you wouldn't get on the radio or the television talking about it like in this country. Sure, if you go to a fair or a town at home and you see strange faces about you can't be certain they *be's* just strangers. Perhaps they could be part of the great Host of the Dead. The strong, silent crowd, as the ould ones call them.

"Och, if it weren't for Wee Kitty sure the lorry would have had me killed and you, Michael, wouldn't be here at all—or only half of you, your father's half.

"And the point of the story is that it was bigotry almost murdered me for, if that Cadgette hadn't such a black heart, I would have jumped on his bit of land as quick as you could turn your fist. Bigotry is a killer."

"So why do they hate the colored people so much?" Mike asked, looking for a clear crisp answer like the ones from the Baltimore Catechism that he was used to.

"Jesus, I was in Washington one time when I was taking care of the Burkes' children. We got off at Union Station and what did I see but a bathroom marked COLORED. God above us, I almost fell over. And in this the land of the free?" Annie shook her head. "Why do they hate the colored people? Well, they need someone to hate. The *Sasanachs*. That's the way of them. Wherever you find *Sasanachs* running things, you'll find hate and bigotry. It's their meat and potatoes, y'know.

"My father used say if we woke upon morning and all the blessed *Sasanachs* was gone from green Fodla's plain, sure we'd be like the hunchback that the *síoganna* took the hump from.

Dancing and singing at the crossroads, we'd have bonfires blazing on the heights, up Cnoc an Mhadaigh and on the summit of the Cloigeann. Oh, Patrick looking down from heaven would think it was the Fionn and the Fianna themselves come back! But he said if the opposite happened and the Gaels disappeared, sure the *Sasanachs* would be full of sorrow for want of us to hate! God above us, the Orangemen and the devilish 'prentices would be marching off the Giant's Causeway into the ocean with their fifes, drums and sashes instead of through Derry. The tide would be filled with their bodies, the poor *créatúrs*, and God have mercy on their souls."

"What would happen if the colored people disappeared from America?" Mike asked.

"Sure, I am not certain at all that the Ku Klux Klan would commit suicide. They'd be after the Jews then and the Cubans and the Porto Ricans, y'know. There's a big selection of people to hate in this country, not like at home at all, where's it only the *Papishes*. They'd be after us too. All us Catholics. They think we've got horns hidden under our hair like Devils. Oh, the *Sasanachs* is great men for the Devil. The ould ones said it was the Cromwell who brought the Devil back into Ireland after Patrick had driven him out."

"How come the Irish-Americans hate the coloreds, Mammy? They're not *Sasanachs*."

"Well, that's a kinda mystery. They say it makes some people feel good about themselves, hating other people, hating different nationalities, looking down on them and the like. I don't believe it. I can't imagine how hate would make you feel good. Jesus, I don't think ould Captain Cadgette ever felt good a day in his life from what Bella Wilson said and him looking out from his big house at the hillsides full of Gaels.

"They're a queer crowd, these Irish-Americans, these narrowbacks. Now don't get me wrong, and America is the greatest country in the world, and where would the rest of the world be if the Americans hadn't won the war, but America changes people and not always for the better. I think it's the food they eat here. Too much red meat entirely. It makes them a bit slow in the head.

"Sure Americans don't know how to work, y'know. If you want a carpentry job done, your father says, it's boys from the other side you want, or Dutchmen or Swedes, great men for the work, them fellas. Not narrowbacks or Americans of any kind. They make *frois frais* of whatever they do. It's many a job our Jimmy has got, repairing damage that Americans have done. Sure, if you look in the paper for a joiner you'll see how they say "European trained" so a person knows the job'll get done right if he hires them. Too much red meat. After a few generations, they lose interest in working. They'd rather stand around and talk about work than do it. That's why they all want to be rich 'cause they've gotten lazy from all that meat. Sure you're better off with cabbage and potatoes and a bit of bacon or ham for taste."

"Where does that leave me, Mammy? Amn't I an American?"

"Och *aidhe*, you are that but not that sort of American. Sure your father and me are not raising a litter of narrowbacks."

Mike had to get dressed for school and the conversation ended. So he had an answer. Red meat. Maybe it was all those steaks and hamburgers that Deucey had eaten in his life, that was why he could hate the coloreds so much that he'd want to blow up the church in the RKO. But maybe it was also because the minister had called him a "bastard."

Mike had been too embarrassed to ask his mother why somebody could get so upset about that word. It had to do with sex and you wouldn't want to be talking to your mother about anything to do with that. Even though people didn't use it that way. It was just a curse word. As far as Mike could see it was a lot worse to be called a "cocksucker" or a "scumbag" than a bastard. But Deucey himself had said he'd rather be called a "cocksucker" than a bastard.

If he was a war hero and a great athlete and a likely successor to Willie the Actor Sutton, there was still something unexplained about him. Like America itself, he was hard to understand. A bit mysterious despite the bright sunshine and blue skies and skyscrapers glistening across the horizon. The whole thing about the dynamite became harder and harder to understand the more he thought about it. For the first time in his life, he could feel a separation arising between himself and the great Deucey Doyle. He didn't appreciate this because Deucey had always been his idol, his escape from the way his family was and what they expected of him.

Well, he thought to himself, if his hero was indeed going to blow up the former RKO at least he wasn't going to do it while the colored people were in it. He'd told Tommy the Hat that he was going to do it at night "so nobody would get hurt," those were his exact words. Deucey wouldn't kill innocent people, women and children, just to get back at the pastor of the church. He was above that. After all, he was an A-1, genuine war hero with medals to prove it. He'd swum through burning water like a son of Uisneach to save his fellow sailors' lives. That proved he had a heart as big as the Philippine Sea itself. He wasn't any Nazi coward who killed babies and women. He didn't even hate colored people. "I don't hate niggers," he'd said and you had to believe him.

If that minister hadn't called him a "bastard" he would have never gotten the idea to blow the place. If only that minister hadn't lost his temper. It was really his fault.

Deucey said he was only going to do it to keep the blacks out of Precious Blood. Maybe he was right, Mike thought. Maybe it would be better if the races didn't mix. There'd be less fights that way. People said things would be better like they were in the old days, when there weren't so many colored people in Brooklyn. They said it would be better if they all stayed down south in Dixie where they belonged. People said they were happier down there. Coloreds didn't go around robbing whites down south. If the coloreds had stayed down south he knew he'd still have that old Joe Medwick Special and he would have never felt the hard point of a blade in his ribs in the dark of the movie house that was now a black church; he would have never felt that feeling of fear that made him shake where you weren't supposed to, deep inside.

MIKE TRIED NOT to stare up at the roof of the RKO as he walked by on his way to school. But he couldn't help but give a few quick glances as he waited for the light to turn green. The dynamite was on his mind.

Precious Blood Church rose lime-white in two towers topped with green bronze like a bit of baroque Spain amid the red brick tenements. Its bells rang out the quarter hours and its clocks lit up gold at night so you could read the time as the black wrought iron hands moved slowly across the faces. The sanctuary of the church was covered with pink marble and over the altar, also of pink marble, was the painting of the Precious Blood, of Christ bleeding from His Wounds. He stood facing the congregation with His arms outstretched and His Holy Blood spurted in jets from the holes in the palms of His hands and in the insteps of His feet and from the diagonal stab wound over His heart and from His forehead where the Crown of Thorns had dug into His skin. Fountains of blood shot out arching like rainbows that fell into cups of silver and gold, chalices held out by long-haired angels and saints. Under them, in gold leaf, *Recolitur memoria Passionis Eius:* May the memory of His Passion be recalled.

Mike prayed against lightning. He knelt at the communion rail and prayed to the bleeding Christ and to Mary, His mother who was easier to talk to, and to Brighid na nGael, the saint with special power against fire and lightning.

BROTHER BAROMETER SLAMMED his yardstick down on his desk to get the class's attention. It was Friday and the boys were even more restless than usual, dreaming of their freedom in the afternoon, full of anticipation about Saturday, that day without limit. No school. No church. Day of stoop-ball, box-ball, day of playground, park, day of double feature, ten cartoons, joyful darkness, ju-jubes sticking in the teeth.

"This weekend, gentlemen, I've got a special assignment for you." He spoke from behind rimless glasses.

The class moved in its seats. Feet shuffled under desks accompanied by low groans.

"I thought you'd appreciate that," he said, smiling sardonically. He stretched out his arms in front of him, intertwining his fingers and cracking his knuckles.

"What I want you to do is read the funnies on Sunday," he continued, still smiling.

Mike laughed, thinking Barometer was pulling his leg, and the others laughed, too.

"I'm serious, gentlemen. After everyone in your family is through reading the funny papers, I want you to go through them with a red pencil and make a large X over every sin you see committed."

There was more disbelieving laughter.

"Are you writing this assignment down? You'll be marked on it!" he announced loudly, maintaining order.

Brother Charles Barometer whose proper name was Charles Borromeo in honor of the sixteenth-century bishop of Milan and Church reformer, was the toughest marker Mike had ever encountered in his seven years at Precious Blood. Barometer would take points off for penmanship even if the answer was correct. You could lose as many points for crossing out something in an arithmetic problem as for getting the wrong answer. The only student who had ever gotten an average higher than 95 percent from Barometer was Eamonn Driscoll, and Mike felt he was paying for this. From the get-go it seemed that the teacher had it in for him. The brother would often refer to Mike as "Eamonn Driscoll's little brother" with a sarcastic tone in his voice. There was an undeclared war between the two. It would have never occurred to Mike to confide in Barometer about the dynamite or any other problem. Brothers were the cops of the soul. Even the nicest ones, he couldn't trust.

Barometer took a piece of pink chalk from the chalk tray and drew a large X on the blackboard.

"Next to each X write a number in numerical order, gentlemen. Transcribe this number onto a sheet of looseleaf and write the name, type and kind of sin next to that number. For example if a character is stealing candy, write *stealing* and then *sin of deed* and then *mortal* or *venial*. Instead of just reading the funnies, I want you to analyze them just as we analyze sentences in grammar—except that here we're talking about sins of deed or sins of thought instead of transitive and intransitive verbs.

"Doyle! What's a mortal sin?" he asked, pointing his pink nub of chalk at Charlie.

"Like murder," Charlie replied. "Thieving big money."

"Those are examples, Doyle. I'm looking for a definition."

"Uh, I dunno, Brudda. I forget."

"I don't understand how you expect to get into Heaven if you don't know these answers. If you don't know what a mortal sin is now when you're in school, how will you know later when you're grown up and out in the world?"

Barometer shook his head in despair.

"Who can give me a definition of mortal sin?"

Vinnie Collucci raised his hand.

"Collucci?"

"Mortal sin is to commit a grievous offense against the law of God."

"Exactly, Vincent. Now, when you're examining the funny papers—and we'll be doing that this Sunday, won't we, Doyle?" he said, sardonically smiling at Charlie, "look out for the following sins: boastful or bragging speech; superstition; disobedience; fighting; murder; quarreling; immodesty in dress, particularly in women; vanity; stealing; damaging property; lying, and of course the seven capital sins of pride, covetousness, lust, anger, gluttony, envy and sloth. Did you get all that?"

"What came after murder?" asked a boy, raising his hand.

"Quarreling."

"After stealing?" asked another.

"What came after stealing, Collucci?" asked Barometer.

"Damaging property," said Vinnie, jumping up from his desk like a soldier of Christ.

"The Seven Deadly Sins?" asked Charlie.

"Look them up in the catechism, Doyle," said Barometer, smiling sarcastically.

"Let's review this week's work, gentlemen," the brother continued. "Who knows the chief punishments of Adam, which we inherit through Original Sin?"

Collucci raised his hand in a flash.

"Collucci?"

"The chief punishments of Adam, which we inherit through Original Sin, are: death, suffering, ignorance, and a strong inclination to sin," said Vinnie, repeating the catechism text word for word.

"Exactly, Vincent," replied Barometer. "Is God unjust, Vincent, in punishing us on account of the sin of Adam and Eve?"

"God is not unjust in punishing us on account of the sin of Adam and Eve because Original Sin does not take anything away from us as human beings to which we have a strict right but only the free gifts that God in his goodness would have bestowed on us if Adam had not sinned."

"Fine, except that you should have said, 'take away from us anything to which we have a strict right as human beings,' and not, 'take anything away from us as human beings . . . ,' as *you* said, Collucci."

Collucci was upset. Mike smiled.

Mike raised his hand.

"And how is Eamonn's little brother today?"

"Fine, Brother. I don't understand why we should be punished just because Adam and Eve ate the apple. Like, we didn't eat the apple, so why do we have to suffer for it?"

"That's why it's called Original Sin, Driscoll. We inherit it, just as we inherit the color of our eyes and the color of our skin and hair from our parents and ancestors."

"But what about the Immaculate Conception?" argued Mike. "If God could let Mary be born without Original Sin, why couldn't he let the rest of us, too?"

"God let the Blessed Virgin be born without sin because she was going to be the Mother Of God! No one else was going to be that important!"

"Well, if God is all-knowing, he could see what was going to happen with the apple, so why didn't he make Adam and Eve stronger so they could have resisted better, so we would not have inherited death and ignorance and the inclination to sin?" Mike was thinking of Deucey and the dynamite. Images of explosions and the word "nigger" crossed his mind.

"Well, who has an answer for Mister Driscoll here?" asked Barometer.

Collucci waved his hand furiously.

"Because of free will," he said springing up like a jack-in-the-box. "He wanted to give Adam and Eve a choice."

"Exactly, Vincent."

Mike shook his head, dissatisfied.

"But if God knew everything that was going to happen because of Original Sin—all the sin and suffering and all—in advance, then why did he bother going ahead with Creation?" asked Mike. "If I was making a boat and I knew it would sink ahead of time, I'd stop building it and build a better one, right?"

Mike looked over at Charlie, who smiled encouragingly and elbowed his neighbor to do the same.

"We don't care what *you* would do, Driscoll," replied Barometer, his eyes flashing angrily from Mike to Charlie. "We're talking about what God did, our Divine Lord and King. Your ideas are useless when talking about God."

"Why did God create us, Vincent?" he asked.

"God created us to know, love and serve Him in this world and the next."

"Exactly! This is what God wants from us, Driscoll. Knowledge, Love and Service."

"I don't understand, Brother. If God loves us so much, why does he bring us into a world full of hate and death and sinful pleasures and then send us to Hell if we give in to temptation?"

"The world is a testing ground, like Los Alamos in New Mexico. Here we prove ourselves. God doesn't send us to Hell. We send ourselves there. All the evils of this world have been created by men, not God!"

"But still, if God knows in advance that someone is going to Hell—and the Gospel says, 'Many are called but few are chosen'—then why does He create a person? If He loved that person, wouldn't be it better to leave him unborn?"

"If you believe that, Driscoll, you're going to Hell yourself! That's the doctrine of predestination, which has been condemned by Holy Mother the Church! The doctrine of John Calvin!"

Barometer left the front of the room and walked down the aisle to Mike's desk. He stood over him threateningly and shook his right index finger in Mike's face as he spoke.

"Do you want to go to Hell, Driscoll?" he asked, sounding each word slowly and ominously.

Mike looked at the long finger and inhaled the odor of aftershave lotion that came from Barometer's black habit. It was as if the air had been drowned. Mike could hardly breathe. His heart pounded.

"Do you want to go to Hell?" repeated the towering voice.

Part of Mike wanted boldly to answer *yes*. *Yes, I want to go to Hell! Yes! Yes! Yes! Just as long as I don't have to listen to you anymore!* But he didn't answer. He felt like he hadn't the spit to produce the words, his mouth was that dry.

"Driscoll, I'm talking to you!" growled Barometer. "Do you want to go to Hell?"

"No," answered Mike with a feeble cough. His voice was small and the word pathetically short in comparison with the thick pointing finger and the overwhelming black of the brother's habit.

"What did you say?" asked Barometer, savoring victory. "Say it so everyone can hear."

"No," repeated Mike.

"No, what?"

"No, Brother."

Vinnie Collucci giggled. Soon everyone was giggling at Mike except his pal, Charlie.

"Believe, Driscoll! Believe!" thundered Barometer. "You're here to know, love and serve God. I recommend that you don't get into waters that are over your head. The devil is everywhere, waiting to pull us down into the depths of Hell. Particularly those who like yourself are puffed up with foolish pride and vanity."

Mike had lost another skirmish in the war of knowledge. Or perhaps it was a victory, getting Barometer to lose his temper. It depended on his mood, the way he saw it. Victory or defeat. But the search for truth was indeed a war at Precious Blood unless you accepted the authorized version of it that was handed to you on a silver communion paten.

For two thousand years great-minded monks and priests had been figuring out all the answers to all the problems of the world. They had even figured out all the questions, there wasn't one square inch of uncertainty left on the face of the Earth even in the vast open spaces of America, for all truth had been gathered and distilled down into the 499 questions and answers in the Baltimore Cathechism. Theology was the Queen of the Sciences and all other disciplines were handmaidens unto her. Reality was a great pyramid rising up to God, and if a student challenged one of the 499 questions or answers, he was attacking the very foundation of this pyramid of revealed truth. Each doubt was seditious. Refusing to bend to the will of the teacher who was the legitimate representative of God in the classroom was treason. Those who doubted were condemned to a spiritual Siberia, which would be followed by the eternal night of damnation.

Thus, when Mike raised his voice, he was taking his eternal life in his hands and there was always, too, the chance that the process of retribution would be swifter and more final, that God the Father would let loose with one of his lightning bolts and strike him down just as lightning could strike the dynamite on the roof of the old RKO Grant and send the whole of Brevoort Street into oblivion. God did things like that and they were called "acts of God" by insurance companies: lightning, forest fires, earthquakes, typhoons and tornadoes, tidal waves.

Thus the attention to detail when Vinnie Collucci was giving the answers. Any deviation from the text, even accidental, could cause misinterpretations to arise and be the occasion of losing souls to Error. There were no "self-evident truths" in the Baltimore Catechism, no reference to "life, liberty and the pursuit of happiness." The first was God-given and the latter two sounded positively sinful. There were no Patrick Henrys in the canon of Catholic saints.

If Mike questioned, he was not a seeker after truth, he was a rebel, a naysayer, a small-time follower of Lucifer, he who would not serve, out of false pride. For the spirit of inquiry was just that, false pride and sinful arrogance.

And if Brother Barometer had the assurance that he was right in persecuting Mike, Mike had no such certainty. What he was doing was called *dornásc* by his father, the process of working in the dark with the hands. There was no assurance, no certainty to it, but Jimmy'd said he'd caught many a trout by *dornásc* under the banks of the river that ran past his hometown. But it was a great burden to be cast in this role of rebel, to carry on a war every time he opened his mouth in class, to be a guerrilla for truth, always on the run from the heavy artillery of orthodoxy. This was especially true when he was feeling unsure and frightened himself, as he was now, worrying about the dynamite on the roof and the kind of a man the great Deucey Doyle really was.

The bell rang at twenty minutes to three, signalling the end of the schoolday. The stairwells echoed as shoe taps struck the corduroy steel of the fire-proof stairs. The roar began on the fourth floor as Mike left the room with the his class. It was like a tiny dot of sound, a sixty-fourth note, a vague tickle in the throat that grew stronger with every step the boys descended toward the front doors. When they hit the fresh air of the street and the sunlight that smashed through the black iron picket fence kissed their faces, it burst out of each mouth like a shooting flame. Roar of each mouth joined roar of its neighbor. Rush down the block. Bookbags flew. Garbage cans tumbled. Empty bottles soared through the air into the headless crowd. Freedom.

AS MIKE AND his classmates were charging through the sunlight, Annie was kneeling in the dark at the back of the church. It was her turn to struggle. She felt giddy in a bad sort of way, as if her knees could no longer carry the weight of her body. She feared she might fold up like an accordion, collapsing with a slow whine into the narrow, insignificant space between the kneeler and the pew.

She'd never attempted anything like what she was doing. Getting a second opinion on sin was not something undertaken every day. Father Murray had turned her down for absolution last week and she was hoping to get a different verdict from Monsignor Shugrue.

Priests were experts on sin, without doubt, as they'd been studying it for years. But for the life of her she couldn't see the harm in using a diaphragm, a thing which was considered sinful by the Church. *Artificial* birth control they called it. They wanted a woman to use the rhythm method, but that didn't work too well. Sure, Mike himself was a rhythm baby. She'd been using the diaphragm for the past five years and it gave her peace of mind. For there was no reason that a person should suffer every time she made love, worrying. Even prophylactics weren't reliable all the time. There was many a surprise visitor hid in those Trojan horses, from what she'd heard other women saying.

She hadn't been absolved in confession for the five years because of the diaphragm. This meant she hadn't been in the state of Grace for all that time and that she couldn't receive communion. She didn't feel like a sinner at all, but it was very embarrassing, particularly on Christmas and Easter when people tended to receive, and noticed who was receiving and who wasn't receiving. Her friend Nancy noticed, of course, and had probably written home about it. Nancy didn't have to worry about such things with Bill drinking so much. He probably didn't remember whether he had or hadn't. Annie was very glad the children didn't go to Mass with her, so she was never embarrassed in front of them. My God, what excuse could she have given to Eamonn, and him wanting to be a priest?

Unlike Mike she was not surprised by the unreasonableness of the Church on this issue. The whole world was unreasonable as far as she could see. Two great wars in thirty years. Millions dead and the Depression in between. Oh, wasn't the world always hard? Why should the Church be any different?

She had hope though that the monsignor would see her point of view. He was an older man, wiser in the ways of the heart. Perhaps, he'd understand her point of view and let her return to the sacraments. If she didn't see herself as a religious person, that didn't mean that she wasn't uncomfortable not being able to do her Easter duty. Of course, her Jimmy could have received communion if he chose for men weren't held responsible for the sin of birth control. It was the woman's body and the woman's sin. But Jimmy hadn't received communion in five years either. God bless him, he said he was out on a "sympathy strike."

The kneeler creaked as she rose and walked down the aisle toward Shugrue's confessional. There was a short line.

A young woman with a yellow kerchief on her head and a toddler next to her was chewing gum while she said her penance. This had to be sacrilegious, Annie thought; it was like chewing the communion host. She wondered what kind of mother this young woman had. She probably spent her time gossiping in front of the ice-cream parlor when she should have been home being useful. Chewing gum, and smoking, and talking to men who weren't her husband. Sure, who's the father of that baby? Her husband or one of those rogues mooching about all day in Santo's Bakery? Playing the horses and pitching pennies. Maybe that Deucey Doyle was the father? Sure, you'd think he had a plate in his head from the war, the way he acted. It was like he never grew up, running 'round robbing stores with a gun! Was that any way for a grown man to be acting, and a war hero on top of it? A bull of a man. Too much red meat.

It was her turn to enter the confessional. It was mahogany and looked like a fancy phone booth. She pulled back the purple drape and knelt in the darkness. A wire grill and a sliding panel separated her from the pastor. He was listening to a confession on the other side. Annie could hear the whispered words but tried not to listen, not wanting to hear the sins of another woman. Mike had told her once that the confessional reminded him of the Automat because suddenly the little door was pulled back and there was the priest, like a tongue sandwich. Annie wondered where he got such notions. The idea made her giggle and added to the strange giddiness she'd experienced since entering the church. She hoped that Father Shugrue didn't hear. Again she felt her knees would give way and she would collapse in the darkness. The panel slipped open.

"Bless me, Father, for I have sinned, it's five years since my last good confession."

"Five years is a long time," the pastor replied.

"It is, Father, and that's what I want to talk about. It's like this. I've been using the diaphragm and I couldn't get absolution and . . ."

"And you've stopped using this mechanical device and want to return to the sacraments," said Shugrue hopefully.

"Sure I'd love to, Father, but that's the thing, we can't afford to. How could we make ends meet if I had another child? We're already bursting out of the place where we are and I'm trying to get my Jimmy to let me work part time. Och, Father, the priests I've talked to, well, they're all young men and I thought that maybe you, being you're an older and have experience of the world, well, I thought . . ."

"How many children do you have?" asked the priest, interrupting.

Annie took heart at the nature of the question. Perhaps there was a right number that would change the clerical opinion.

"Three," she replied hopefully.

"Three is no great amount," he replied, "I'm sure you could afford another."

"No, we can't, Father, at all."

"How many children did your mother have?"

"Nine."

"Well then, you know it can be done."

"It can, Father. But we had a farm, Father. It isn't the same thing at all. Sure, you can't be feeding children porridge over here and be letting them run around without shoes. Sure, America isn't Ireland, Father."

"Earthly goods are unimportant," answered Shugrue. "God is not interested in economics. Remember what Our Savior the Lord Jesus Christ said: 'What doth it profit a man if he gain the whole world and lose his immortal soul?'"

"Och Father, we're not trying to gain the whole world at all. We're only trying to hold on to the little we've got. Everything's getting more and more expensive."

"I understand that. But isn't a human soul worth giving up a Sunday roast for?"

"No doubt, Father, and I see what you're saying. But sure a child is more expensive than a Sunday roast."

"It's the principle of the thing," replied the pastor adamantly. "You must allow God to provide."

Annie felt herself getting angry, for the pastor, like all the rest, was turning a deaf ear to her request.

"In regard to principles, Monsignor," she said, "can you explain it to me, why it's a sin to be using a diaphragm and not a sin to be using the rhythm method?"

"Well, rhythm is approved by the Church because it does not interfere with nature while the diaphragm does. You see the diaphragm is artificial and therefore *unnatural* and sinful, while rhythm is not artificial but *natural* and therefore not sinful."

"But the thing I'm asking is, Father, does it make any difference what method I use if it's *not* trying to have a child I am?

Amn't I sinning as well with the rhythm as I'm not looking for God to bless the union?"

"Well, I'm glad to hear that you remember that the married couple should pray to God for their union to be blessed," said Shugrue in a condescending tone. "There is a difference. A real difference. It is still possible to have a child when you use the rhythm method. The union then can be blessed by God. That's the essence of the thing."

"Oh, I'm expert on that subject for me youngest boy is the result of the rhythm, you see." She spoke loudly, clothing her anger in a tone of humble irony.

Shugrue was taken aback for he felt he'd been led into a trap but he quickly recovered.

"And don't you love him?" he asked greedily. "And aren't you glad he was born? And wouldn't your be heart broken if he was taken from you?"

"It would, Father, without doubt. But I don't know if I'd feel the same if I'd five others for every year I've been kept from the sacraments."

She controlled her temper. She'd never heard of a priest who didn't live well in this country or in the old. Sunday dinners every night they had, according to Nancy, whose friend Delia cooked in the rectory at Precious Blood. And they'd an elevator that went from the basement to the third floor, a little elevator that fit two people. And they'd put it in during the Depression when everybody was out of work!

"I just don't understand at all, Father," she said, her voice filled with frustration.

"Pray for faith," replied the pastor, exultant in his victory over this upstart countrywoman. "The way of faith leads to truth. Whereas the road of reason often leads us astray. That is the paradox."

Annie wanted to look into his eyes but she could barely make out his features in the dim light of the confessional. If only he could see into hers, he might understand her plight, she thought. Her fear, her anxiety. Perhaps that was reason they made confessionals so dark, so that priests would not have to see.

"Well, Father, we just can't afford to use rhythm. We want our children to live better than we did when we were young."

"Of course I can't give you absolution under those conditions," he said impatiently.

"I know that, Father. But could you give forgiveness for my other sins like anger and such?"

"No, I can't," he snapped. "Penance is all of one piece. You can't bargain with God. He is not a merchant."

Annie didn't answer. She had nothing more to say.

"Pray for faith. I repeat, pray for faith," said Shugrue, closing the sliding door and disappearing completely from view.

She knelt in the darkness for a few moments to collect herself before leaving the confessional and facing the world. She wiped her nose with a handkerchief, a small white square of cloth that smelled of perfume. More smell in it than in the entire convent, Mike had once said. For the first time since she entered the church her knees felt solid beneath her. She cleared her throat, stood up and left the darkness behind.

JIMMY CAME HOME that night with his middle finger wrapped in a piece of cloth. One of the table saws at Corrigan's had cut a half inch into the bone before the pain had hit him. Annie told him to go the hospital and get it looked after and he answered that he'd be fine and she had to raise her voice and let a tear run down her cheek before he would comply.

Mike and Eamonn accompanied him to the emergency room. Mike felt very important sitting there amid life's casualties. The doctors cleaned and bandaged the finger with a splint and gave his father a tetanus shot. His father smiled and talked through the whole process, asking the nurses and doctors about themselves and their families and where they came from. It was as if he was there on a visit instead of being hurt. Mike could never figure his father out except that he embarrassed him. None of the other patients were gabbing away like him, they were acting like patients should, quiet and pain-full.

"Two years ago it was me little toe was broken," Jimmy said to the doctor who was wrapping his finger up. "Last year I got a splinter of metal in me eye and now it's me finger. Oh, that's the way it is when you work with your hands, a little bite is taken out of you every year. Twenty years from now there won't be anything left of me at all!"

MIKE COULDN'T SLEEP that night. Every time he closed his eyes he'd see visions of his father being eaten up by a high-speed saw or images of the dynamite exploding and blowing the RKO, and Brevoort Street, sky high full of bloody limbs. He prayed to God to keep his father from further harm and to Brighid to keep fire and lightning from the dynamite. But the dynamite wouldn't let him sleep. There was no way he could unburden himself to his parents about the dynamite without squealing on Deucey and Bunny and of course there was nothing under the wheels of the sun worse than a squealer.

He lay in his bed and could hear his parents talking in the living room, their voices coming clearly through the crack in the door along with a thin blade of light.

"Well, what is it then?" his father said. "What's on you?"

"It's not me, it's you," she replied. "Can't you see you *be's* working too hard. Sure, you almost cut the finger off yourself tonight. Two jobs is too much for a man to be working. Now, if you wasn't . . ."

"Stop right now, woman. I'm all right and if you want to start talking about getting yourself a job then you'll be talking to yourself for I won't be listening to you."

"Och Jimmy, we need the money and you shouldn't be killing yourself, to make it."

"I'm not killing meself. Accidents happen and if you work with a saw you're bound to hurt yourself once in a while."

"You shouldn't need to have two jobs," she said.

"Right you are and if I could get full-time work at Corrigan's, I wouldn't."

"I know that but even if you got full-time work there we would still need more money. Things is getting more expensive every day."

"Well, maybe if you managed better we wouldn't need it," he snapped.

"Listen to him give out! Manage better? And who is it that turns his nose up at leftovers and frankfurters?"

"Frankfurters aren't food, woman. They're for eating in the park like Cracker Jacks. Would you call Cracker Jacks food?"

"Don't we eat better in this house than any other house in the building?" she asked angrily.

"Don't be shouting now!" barked Jimmy. "Do you want all the neighbors to be hearing our business?"

"It's you who's screeching, not meself! All I want is a part-time job! How else are we going to get a bigger apartment? Sure Peggy's becoming a woman already and she can't be sleeping with her brothers too much longer."

"Part-time job! I'll not have the neighbors saying Jimmy Driscoll can't provide for his family."

"Och, man, what are you saying? Sure Nancy works, and Mrs. Collucci and Eileen Evans, too."

"If Bill Doyle didn't spend so much money in the beergarden there'd be little call for Nancy to work, and Collucci spends his money on the horses and those pigeons he raises on the roof. Eileen Evans. It's little I know and care less where she works!"

"Little you care about Eileen Evans? *Muise!*" scoffed Annie. "Every time you see her your eyes get as big as moons in your head!"

"Well, maybe if you hadn't put on two stone weight I wouldn't be looking like that, at all!"

149

"Two stone weight, is it? Listen to him. *Arú*, amn't I but five pounds heavier than the day I first met you?"

"All right, all right. If you want the money so bad, I'll go to work in the Navy Yard. Twelve hundred dollars more in the year. Sure we can get a bigger place and two weeks in the Catskills as well."

"Over my dead body you'll work in the Navy Yard!" she yelled. "You know I don't want you working there! It's to torment me you're saying it!"

MIKE WOKE VERY early the next morning. He found his father sleeping in the bathtub. A pillow squeezed behind his back, his head resting on his wounded bandaged hand and his naked, snow white, blue-veined feet coming out from under the blanket cramped up against the tile wall. He looked pale and strangely fragile, like Christ in the Tomb in the painting under the choir loft in Precious Blood. There was nothing between him and death but the airless barrier of time.

WHEN MIKE WAS listening to his parents argue, his friend Charlie was listening for his father. His mother was in bed and his brother Terry had cut out as soon as it became clear that Bill had stopped off at the bar on his way home from work.

"He'll be okay if he sticks with the beer," Charlie had told his brother hopefully.

"You're livin' in a dream," Terry had replied. "If he stuck wit' the beer he wouldn't be our old man! I'm goin' to Uncle Deucey's for the night."

Charlie didn't blame his brother for leaving because it was him that their father went after when he was loaded. He would have liked to have gone with Terry but he felt he had to stay to protect his mother. Of course he didn't say this to himself, what he kept repeating was, "Maybe he'll stay with the beer. If he stays with the beer, he's not so bad. If he stays with the beer, he's not so bad."

When he heard his mother go to bed, Charlie got up and put on the late show on the television. He had the sound turned way down so that it wouldn't wake her. It was barely audible but it gave him comfort to hear the whispering voices and watch the characters move gracefully across the thirteen-inch screen, their faces so alive even if only in tones of black, white and grey. He loved the movies, and when he got bigger he was going to become an usher like his uncle had suggested. He'd follow in the Great Deucey's footsteps. Of course he couldn't be one in the Grant anymore, since the niggers had taken it over, but maybe in the RKO Savoy or in the Loewies. He'd have a cool uniform and a silver flashlight to flick around in the darkness. Even Peggy Driscoll might fall for him then. He lay there in the dark of the living room, his body washed in the light of the television, this modern moon, and watched and listened as the hero beat the odds and got the girl to boot, and waited for the sound of his father at the door.

He turned off the TV when he heard the key scraping across the lock and retreated to the bedroom. He knew it would take his father a while to get the key in the opening. It was some-thing a drunk couldn't do. He mimicked deep sleep and called it "playing dead." His father was in the kitchen, cursing. He heard the door of the icebox bang against the wall. The old man would be coming to the bedroom soon. He heard him crossing the living room. He tripped on the leg of the coffee table as he always did, and cursed.

The door of the bedroom flew open and banged against the corner of the dresser.

"Where is the fucker?" his father screamed, looking down at Terry's empty bed, made visible by the dim yellow of the street light. "Punk! Out fuckin' around! Runnin' the whores! He's probably gettin' more than I am, the wiseass."

He turned toward Charlie. He lay not breathing, playing dead as best as could. His father's breath filled the room like a sticky sweet tide in which he felt he would soon drown. He wished the old man would hit him and get it over with. He turned toward the wall and braced himself as the fists came down on him again and again. He made like he didn't feel it, like he was sleeping through it, locking his jaw. The blows didn't seem to hurt like they once had. The old man was losing his stuff, he thought. His father left him alone after a couple of barrages. He staggered out of the room and headed back to the kitchen. Charlie heard him searching for a church key to open his quart of Rheingold. Then he heard him going toward his parents' room. Mumbled voices through the thick plaster wall. The bedsprings creaked loudly and his mother gave out a short yelp like a dog whose foot got stepped on.

BILL O'SULLIVAN

. . .

THE CALIFORNIA AIR was clear. Blue sky met slate-colored mountains behind Alan Ladd's cap, which was also blue, with a silver insignia the size of a fifty-cent piece reflecting the bright morning light. He stood in a row of newly graduated jet pilots all dressed in sky blue uniforms with silver insignia shining. They were silent and solemn, with expressions on their faces like people at Mass during the consecration. Alan Ladd looked very calm and determined and he lived off-base with his beautiful wife, June Allyson, who looked harried around the eyes all the time, like she was smoking an invisible cigarette. Nancy Mac Orraistín had that look, too, around the eyes, Mike thought, even when she was laughing. He looked at Charlie who was munching on nonpareils.

"California," said Charlie. "That's where we gonna go. My father says he might be able to get a transfer to the Navy Yard at San Diego. Everybody's happy out there, y'know. Sunshine. They got houses out there, even regular people, with palm trees in the backyard. Evvybody's happy out there. Evvybody."

"Congratulations, gentlemen," said James Whitmore. "You have your jet wings. You are jet pilots."

Mike imagined himself with wings like some military angel as he zoomed the upper reaches of the stratosphere. June Allyson's eyes, blue eyes, and a jet streaking through the blue sky.

"These babies are your firing platforms," said Whitmore, pointing at a row of silver Sabre jets sparkling in the desert air. "They bring you within range of the enemy so you can destroy him. And that's what it's all about, gentlemen. Destroying the enemy."

Shouts of approval erupted from the candy darkness of the Loewies. Foot stomping.

"Kill the fuckin' Nips!" shouted Charlie, banging his feet against the chair in front of him.

"You will be getting your orders for Korea tomorrow. You'll be leaving your wives and loved ones."

June Allyson's blue eyes filled with enormous silver tears at the news.

"Here along the mighty Yalu River!" said Whitmore, slapping the map with a stainless steel pointer.

China was like an enormous red mass from which the peninsula of Korea hung like an empty yellow sock.

Commie pilots vomited red mouthfuls of ketchup before their burning planes spun to deserved destruction. The Sabre jets dove and dropped Technicolor bombs on grey-green mountains and ratty villages. Leathernecks cheered as the napalm enveloped "gook" positions, sending Chicom soldiers into fiery oblivion. Mike and Charlie cheered, imagining themselves as members of Ladd's squadron. But in the midst of one bombing raid, Mike grew silent. He suddenly remembered about the dynamite on the roof of the colored church, on the roof of a movie house similar to the one he was sitting in.

He looked up in dread at the ornately decorated ceiling. Up until that time he had forgotten completely about the explosives and about Deucey and Bunny and Tommy the Hat. Perhaps it had been the sight of his father in the tub that put it from his mind. But from then on, every time a bomb burst on the great silver screen, he quivered. He no longer saw the body parts of evil Commies flying through the black swirling clouds but the limbs of little colored kids and women in flowery dresses. He even saw his own building go up and he saw his mother's pocketbook and his father's milk white feet sailing through the smoke.

Mike had to tell somebody about the dynamite. Its lonely knowledge was killing him.

He hadn't spoken to his friend about it before because, even though it frightened him, he rather enjoyed being in on a secret that Charlie didn't know about for once, particularly one that concerned the great Deuce. Mike had always been jealous of Charlie having an uncle like Deucey. All his uncles were only names in a faraway land. Shadowy presences behind ploughs, in dark boats. To have a hero uncle, that was power.

On the way home from the movies, Mike told his friend about the dynamite. He saw Charlie's eyes grow wide as he unfolded the tale and felt very important, as if he were not merely telling a story but in on the action itself.

"Did you see the stuff?" asked Charlie.

"No."

"You mean you knew the dynamite was up there and you didn't go up to see it?" asked Charlie. "Boy!"

Mike shrugged his shoulders.

"Let's go up there now," said Charlie.

It was Saturday and there was no way that they could climb the fire escape on the side of the old RKO without being seen, so they decided they'd have to jump from the roof of the building next door. The vestibule door was locked so they rang a bell, and when the door buzzed open they yelled up they were looking for Joey, and when the lady who rang the buzzer yelled back there was no Joey, they pretended to leave but stayed inside and kept quiet until the coast seemed to be clear.

They climbed the steps then, trying not to make the steps squeak, which was hard in these old buildings. They didn't talk and pretended to be commandos like they'd seen in the movies.

There was about four feet of space between the two roofs but it looked like the Grand Canyon to Mike when he looked down. Charlie was already on the other roof by the time Mike got up the nerve to spring from the wall. Like his uncle, he was fearless. Mike's heart stopped as he leaped over the abyss. The sole of his sneaker touched the other wall and he bounced forward until he felt the warm softness of the tar under his feet.

The roof of the RKO rose in a great hump like the back of a whale. They couldn't see any dynamite at first. They made their way around to the other side and there it was under a piece of grey tarpaulin. The boxes were of heavy wood like soda crates. The top box was open and they could see the sticks of dynamite lying in there like huge firecrackers.

"I betcha you're afraid to touch one," said Charlie.

"No, I'm not," replied Mike, lying.

"I dare you," said his friend, taunting him.

"You do it if you're so brave," Mike replied.

"Okay," said Charlie and, without a moment's hesitation, he put his hand into the box and picked up one of the sticks.

It was that Doyle courage again, Mike thought. Truly a race of heroes.

"Here, look at it," said Charlie, holding out the stick of dynamite toward Mike.

It took an effort of will for Mike to reach out for the explosive and his hand almost stopped when he got within an inch of it. He had to force it to continue the motion. He thought his fingers were quivering and his knees knocking together when he finally grabbed hold of the dynamite.

Nothing exploded. No shock was received from touching this dangerous, powerful, stolen stuff. Soon he was tossing it from one hand to the other in a show of bravery for Charlie's benefit, trying to make up for his initial hesitation. Oh, but it didn't matter, for he knew he didn't have the boldness of heroes. The boldness in the marrow of all the great heroes from Cú Chulainn down to Colin Kelly, who sank the first Jap battleship single-handed before crashing into the sea back in '42. Heroes didn't think, they did. They didn't worry like he did. Maybe he should be an engineer, as his father wanted, working with a slide rule not a gun.

The boys put back the dynamite and looked out over the neighborhood. There was a pleasant breeze and the West was showing signs of redness against a sky that was no longer blue but light green, like a lime rickey. Tree crowns burst up over the flat sea of black tar roofs. Mr. Collucci's pigeons flew circles round the towers of Precious Blood. The Williamsburgh Bank rose thirty stories over downtown Brooklyn and behind it the metal uprights of the Manhattan Bridge headed for the Bowery and Chinatown. The cranes of the Navy Yard were clear and distinct against the heavens. Charlie said that the carrier *Franklin* was in, getting refitted.

"The carrier that Deucey was on?" asked Mike with eyes wide.

"The hero ship," said Charlie proudly. "The ship the Japs couldn't sink. My father's working on her."

"Think we can get a pass to see her?" asked Mike.

"Sure, when they're finishing up the job. It'll take at least a year, from what my dad says. Maybe I can get my uncle Deucey to come with us and show us around, where he used to sleep and stuff."

"Boy, that'll be great."

There were two destroyers and a heavy cruiser in, as well. Charlie pointed out their conning towers rising up on the horizon. They looked peaceful and natural like delicate grey plants branching up at the edge of the sloping, building-crowded, sea-squeezed borough. Tugboats tooted their horns and the Statue of Liberty raised her lamp behind the elevated line that climbed out of the earth like a mythical snake.

Mike looked over at the boxes of dynamite.

"Do you really think your uncle will blow up the place?" he asked.

"If he said he would, he'll do it. Teach the niggers a lesson."

"They ain't done anything to us," objected Mike.

"Didn't they steal your baseball glove? Wasn't it a coon who tried to hold you up right here in the Grant?"

"My parents say it's because they think we got money. They think all white people are rich or something."

"I don't give a shit what they think. My old man says coons is gonna take over the country if we don't watch it. Coons, kikes and Commies."

The bells of Precious Blood rang out the quarter hour. Mr.

Collucci's pigeons rose up and mushroomed out around the tower like an A-bomb of beating wings.

THE NEXT DAY, Sunday, was extremely warm. The radio said that the heat was breaking all records for the date. A threat of "severe thunderstorms" was forecast for the evening. Mike had never paid much attention to the weather forecasts previously (except for predictions of glorious blizzards that might close Precious Blood School) but when he heard the word "thunderstorm" he felt himself quake inside, that same horrid shaking feeling he'd felt when the colored kid had held the knife to his ribs. He was remembering the great Deucey's remark that only lightning could set off the dynamite. Lightning, and here it was, predicted for the evening. The colored people spent all day Sunday in the church too; they had services going till the evening. He hoped to God that Deucey was listening to the radio. Maybe he'd move the dynamite if he heard? But how could he move it in broad daylight and with all those people milling about? Visions of exploded bodies filled his head. Mike found it hard to contain his fear and he kept asking his parents if they thought there'd be storms like the radio said.

"Jesus, you'd think he had sheep on the mountain the way he's going on," said Annie to Jimmy, casting a suspicious glance over at Mike.

"I was just wonderin'," said Mike, with pretended casualness. Of course he couldn't tell his parents what he really was worrying about. They'd call the cops for sure and that would be the end of his reputation on Brevoort Street. He'd have the name of a squealer.

After an early dinner of pot roast his parents announced they were all going to the Botanical Gardens to see the cherry blossoms and the Doyles were coming along. Mike was wearing his Sunday suit and he asked his mother if he could change into his dungarees. She said he'd do nothing of the kind and he wasn't going to running around like a maniac. They were going for a Sunday stroll and that meant Sunday clothes and behaving like a gentleman.

There were hundreds of Japanese at the front gates of the Botanix that afternoon. Hundreds more were coming up from the subway, smiling, with cameras hanging round their necks.

"There oughta be a law against these people coming to this country," said Bill Doyle. "After Pearl Harbor, who'd rent them an apartment?"

"Jews, probably," he said, answering his own question. "They'd rent Hitler an apartment if they could make money on it."

"Oh, I feel sorry for them all," said Annie. "After Hiroshima and Nagasaki. Did you know they dropped the bomb in Nagasaki on a Catholic seminary? Did you know that?"

"The Masons was behind that, no doubt," said Nancy.

Mike found it hard to imagine that these people who were taking pictures of flowers were the same ones who'd flown kamikazes against the *Franklin* in the Philippine Sea, that sank so many ships at Okinawa. Weren't the Japs the ones who threw themselves from cliffs, who made bayonet charges against the machine guns? If an Irish guy went around taking pictures of flowers, people would say he was a quiff. He tried to imagine what these Jap men would look like wearing uniforms and carrying long samurai swords. They used to bayonet babies in the Philippines and here they were taking photos of flowers and smiling. He'd never seen people smile so much as the Japanese.

"The Japanese are great men for nature," said Jimmy. Every tree or bush that the Japanese would stop to photograph he would stop at. "That picture over our bed, that was made by Japanese. Not a dot of paint in the whole thing. It's made entirely of butterfly wings. Isn't that something now? Oh, it's clever people they are."

"You always said it was Chinese," protested Mike. It had always been a favorite of his and he felt put out to discover that the Japs had done it.

"Japanese? Chinese? What's the difference?" said Jimmy.

"True. All the peoples of the Eastern World are great for nature," said Annie.

"There's a big difference between the Japs and the Chinese. They don't speak the same language. And the Koreans are different again," explained Eamonn.

"They should drop the bomb on the Chinese," said Bill. "After all we did for them and they go Commie."

"When I was a *cailín* they used to spell Korea with a 'C'," Annie said. "It was C-O-R-E-A. There was different countries then, too. Austria-Hungary and the Ottoman Empire. Do you remember that, Jimmy?"

"I remember it. *Muise* there was no Ireland on the maps then either. It was all Great Britain in those days."

161

"No Free State. No Republic then," said Annie.

"Do you see how the Masons are keeping Ireland out of the United Nations?" said Nancy. "Keeping out Spain, too. They don't want too many Catholics countries, afraid they might lose control."

"Do you remember John Mac Loingsigh who went high up in the phone company? From out Rúscaí way he was, Annie?" asked Nancy.

"Oh, I do."

"He died last year up in the Bronx and I went to his wake, for he was related to my mother's people. Well, we were just after saying the rosary for his soul when who would show up but a crowd of them in aprons."

"Masons?" asked Annie.

"Right you are. In the flesh. Oh, it was all very clear then how he got the promotions. A turncoat. You can't get above foreman in the phone company without being a Mason."

"Oh, that's true," said Jimmy. "I was told that when I got off the boat in New York. There's only so high an Irishman can go with the phone company before the Masons will approach him."

"If you become a Mason," said Eamonn, "it means you're excommunicated from the Church, and if you die you go to hell."

"Well, it's a warm welcome the ould buck'll be gettin' in the next world," said Jimmy.

"Didn't the Black Liams go high in the phone company, Nancy?" asked Annie.

"The Black Liams from Buluba?"

"Yes, the ones that the *créachta* followed."

"Not at all. There was a man of the Black Liams who worked for the Edison Company in Philadelphia," replied Nancy. "But the *créachta* didn't strike the Black Liams. It's the Needlers you're thinking of. And it wasn't the phone company they went with but the steel in Pittsburgh. The *créachta* struck them hard. Joe the Needler's people particularly."

The *créachta* was what they called tuberculosis. Sometimes they called it the "decline."

"Are you sure?" asked Annie. "It was the Needlers, was it?"

"The Niall Mac Orraistíns is sib to them."

"'Tis right you are, Nancy. 'Twas Andrew that died first, then Mairéad and Sorcha. All in one year."

"Well, it wasn't Andrew who died first but Mairéad. Then came Andrew and then Róisín. Sorcha didn't die at all," said Nancy.

"All in one year," said Annie, disregarding her friend's corrections.

"If you can call it that," replied Nancy. "Twelve months it was but it was two years by the calendar. Mairéad went in August, Andrew in December and Róisín in July of the next year."

"They got short lives. God's Grace on their souls and the souls of all the dead."

"It was a queer thing how the 'decline' would strike one family and then skip over the next and then strike another," said Nancy.

"Like a fly lighting here and there," said Annie, agreeing. "To think all these years I was thinking that Sorcha was dead.

And what became of her? Did she go out to Pittsburgh to the others?"

"No, she went up to Dublin to study nursing, she did," said Nancy. "And wouldn't you know that the girl who was in the next bed to her was struck by the *créachta* and she didn't know it herself until it was too late."

"Och, that's awful."

"She died."

"Sorcha?"

"No, her that had the decline," said Nancy, testy. "Her people were from the South. Way up in Cork somewhere."

"So the *créachta* never struck Sorcha?"

"No."

"Praise be to God."

"She had an excellent constitution, Sorcha did."

"And is she up in Dublin still?"

"Ach no. She's in Australia these many years."

"Ahh!"

"She went to Liverpool as a nurse and she met an Australian there, she did. He'd broken his leg."

"Poor man," said Annie sympathetically.

"Oh, he wasn't at all," replied Nancy. "*Muise* he was rich. And he carried her off to his cattle station out there and his leg still in a cast. That's what they call ranches, cattle stations."

"Sounds like the subway," joked Bill.

"Sure, isn't that romantic!" sighed Annie, ignoring the wisecrack.

"Och, but he died soon after," sighed Nancy. "And she had two of a family by him."

"He got a short life," said Annie. "'Tis a pity, it is."

"That may be. But Sorcha's rich now. A rich widow woman. There are worse things to be."

"There's no cure for death but marry again," said Jimmy, quoting the proverb.

"Well, the Needlers always knew how to take of themselves as regards money," said Annie.

"Right you are without doubt. But they've had more than their share of tragedy. Don't you know that cousins to our Needlers from Ardán Donn died out in Philadelphia? Three of them within two years, it was."

"Calendar years?" asked Annie facetiously.

"Let me see now," replied Nancy, disregarding the intent. "It was in '38, '39 and '40."

"Was it the *créachta?*"

"Not at all. It was 'lectricity."

"'Lectricity, was it? And how's it they died of that?"

"I'll tell you. The oldest brother John James worked for the Edison Company in Philadelphia . . ."

"Where the man of the Black Liams worked?" asked Annie, interrupting.

"Exactly, but I don't think they worked together. Now John James got his youngest brother a job there too, and they worked alongside on the high tension wires."

"So that's how they died. High tension was it?"

"Right you are. John James in the summer of '38. And young *stocach* Séarlus died in January of '39."

"God save us all! And who was the third brother?"

"It wasn't a brother. It was Deirdre, God rest her."

"The 'lectric company, too?" asked Annie surprised.

"*Arú,* it was a toaster that killed her."

"Mother of God, do you hear this? A toaster. And how did it happen?"

"Sure, she was wiping it off and it fell into a sink full of water! And like an *amadán,* she plunged her hands into the water after it and the water was 'lectrified and the shock killed her!"

"God between us and all harm! The toaster must have been 'on' at the time. Sure what was doing wiping it off and it 'on'?"

"A very tidy woman about the house," replied Nancy.

"She was that," said Annie.

"Well, it's certain that the 'lectricity followed that crowd of Needlers in Philadelphia," declared Nancy. "And the *créachta* got those in Rúscaí."

"There's a *tubaisce* on the Needlers for sure," said Annie darkly.

"The decline and the 'lectricity," said Nancy, nodding in agreement.

"Do you remember that picture with George Raft and Marlene Dietrich?" said Jimmy.

"*High Voltage,*" said Bill.

"No, it was *Manpower* and Edward G. Robinson was the star," said Eamonn. "I saw it last year at the Itch."

The Itch was a re-run movie house in the neighborhood.

"They don't be making pictures about workingmen anymore," said Jimmy. "Do you remember all those pictures about truck drivers and oil drillers!"

"Indeed I do," replied Nancy wistfully. "Those were grand pictures."

"Grand they were," added Annie. "Why don't they make pictures like that anymore?"

"They've no interest in workingmen anymore," said Jimmy. "Och, the trades are all dying out. Soon there won't be any left. That's why I tell Michael here to go with the engineering. They'll always need roads and bridges."

"They say in fifty years that machines will be doing all the work," said Bill. "There won't be any work for people anymore. Jesus, I'm glad I won't be alive."

"Does it look that bad to you?" asked Jimmy.

"Worse," said Bill. "Worse."

"Look at yon bush," said Annie. "Isn't it grand?"

Mike felt trapped in his Sunday clothes. The starched collar of his sports shirt irritated his neck even though it wasn't buttoned up to the top. The threat of the storm and the fear of the dynamite made him uneasy.

"Do you think it'll blow?" he asked Charlie.

"Naw, don' worry about it," his friend replied. "Even if there is lightning, it would be like hitting a needle in a haystack."

"Smile, *Micilín*. Smile," said Annie, lining them up for a photo under a cherry tree in full blossom. "Look at the *púic* on him, Nancy."

He didn't feel like smiling. The whole neighborhood might blow up in a couple of hours and she wanted him to smile. The world was much simpler before the dynamite. He didn't have this worry then. He wished he'd never seen Deucey coming out of the alleyway. He wished he hadn't been so damn inquisitive. If he hadn't gone into the Joy, he wouldn't have heard. It would have been simpler then, without this knowledge. He could have run through the Botanix feeling free like he had often done before, his mother screaming at him to mind his suit.

He couldn't squeal. No matter how bad it got, he couldn't squeal. He was no squealer, no stoolpigeon, no informer. Look what happened to squealers. Arnold Schuster.

He and Charlie walked over to the small stream that flowed through the length of the Botanical Gardens. A few years before he'd captured a tadpole in this water and brought it home in a mayonnaise jar. Over the next week he'd watched it change from a dark fishlike creature into a tiny frog. The process had left him full of wonder and amazement. He doubted that life could ever hold such simple wonder again because of the dynamite. He looked in the water for tadpoles, for the tiny crayfish that also lived there. There weren't any to be seen. He bent down and put his hand into the current. It ran through his fingers, cool and pleasant. He wished they'd rent a row boat and go out on Prospect Lake. He would take his dress black shoes off and his socks and roll up the legs of his pants and sit in the back of the boat and let his feet dangle into the water while his father rowed them about as he had done in past years. Suddenly the vision shifted and his father was no longer in a boat but straddling the lid of a coffin and it was his milk white feet in the water and not Mike's. They were in the middle of a sea of rising and falling coffins, an ocean crowded with caskets bumping each other, opening like jacks-in-the-box and colored bodies bouncing out of them and white bodies, his mother and his brother and his sister and Charlie and Bill and Nancy and Bunny Imp and

Tommy the Hat and Brother Barometer all leaping with accordion bodies. The cheeping of the birds became the screeching of dying children and the stream turned red like in a prophecy of Colmcille.

"Beat you to the Japanese Garden," yelled Charlie, running off. Mike took off after him.

The Japanese Garden was separated from the rest of the Botanix by a bamboo fence over six foot high. There was a special entrance with a turnstile although there was no charge to get in. They were keeping count. But why? This was a mystery. The whole place felt mysterious and different. There was the Red Gate that rose out of the lake without a building or house behind it. It was gate to nowhere or nothing with big black Japanese letters above.

"They're ideograms," declared Eamonn but even he didn't know what they meant.

They stood in the wooden pagoda that extended out over the lake with its slanting roof and rising eaves and its floor of yellow wooden slats through which Mike could see the water trembling. There were goldfish in the lake. Huge goldfish and catfish, too, with ugly snouts and whiskers. They walked the path that skirted the water to a shrine amid rocks. The Japanese with cameras were all smiling as if they recognized the place and shaking their heads as if embarrassed.

Annie said if it had been home in the ould country, there would be *síoganna* living in such a place.

"Don't give us that Irish malarkey," said Bill, scornfully.

Peggy was standing by the water putting on lipstick. "I think I'm going to vomit," she announced, pretending to gag.

"Are you afraid one of your friends will see you with us?" asked Annie sarcastically.

"My friends have no time for the Botanical Gardens. I mean it's so dumb!" she replied.

"Oh Jesus, nothin' but Jews and Japs," sighed Bill. "What's happenin' to old Brooklyn?"

They weren't regular Jews. They were called Loobavitchas, from down Eastern Parkway they were. Black hats and black coats and long beards on the men. The women wore kerchiefs to cover their hair, or wigs, because of their religion. (Benny of the candy store had explained it to Mike and he knew because he was Jewish, regular Jewish, normal.) All the boys wore yarmulkes and had shaved heads like they'd just escaped from a concentration camp except they had long ugly banana curls hanging down in front of their ears. Even though it was hot and the sun was shining they looked sickly; that was because they spent all their days behind bibles, according to Benny, in dark libraries. Some of the men were wearing knee-breeches and white stockings like stage Irishmen except they didn't have green hats with gold buckles. They had hats that looked like furry flying saucers. They talked nervously and looked harried, their eyes searching around as if expecting disaster. Mike knew how they felt. He looked up into the sky, fearful of black clouds. Three families of Loobavitchas filled the entire pagoda so that it seemed to creak. Annie was waiting for it to collapse under their weight. She'd never seen so many children. Monsignor Shugrue would be very happy with them, she thought. She couldn't imagine what you would do with all those children in the heart of the city.

The hothouse looked like a glass cathedral or circus tent with its translucent cupola rising. Tropical flowers inside and palm trees thirty feet tall. It was even stickier inside than out, so that Annie let Mike take off his suit jacket. Orchids and rubber. Rose of Venezuela. Flame of the Forest. Sound of water drip-dropping.

Out of the Botanix into the Zoo. Its air filled with lion roar and elephant shit. The Zoo made Peggy cry so she sat under the statue of the she-wolf that had fed Romulus and Remus with her pointy tits. Seals clapped. Odor of frankfurters and Cracker Jacks near the merry-go-round. Chariots drawn by mustard-colored lions. His father asked him and Charlie if they wanted to ride. They made faces and said they were too old. Mike envied the young children as he watched the horses rising and falling on the tile poles. Joyful faces. He remembered his father holding him on a horse when he was very little. The feel of the carved mane in his fingers was unmistakable. He felt tears in his eyes. God, he thought, he was getting like Peggy. He turned away quickly and ran so no one would see.

They went to the beergarden across the way on Empire Boulevard. It was a real beergarden with a yard shaded by a tree and wooden tables and benches where people sat drinking their beer and talking and eating sandwiches.

"Only beer, Bill," Mike heard Nancy whisper.

"I promise, hon'," said Bill.

The adults drank from a pitcher of beer while the children drank Cokes. Mike loved it. The Cokes had ice cubes in them that had holes in the center. He and Charlie kept sticking them on the tips of their tongues and upsetting Peggy, who threatened to vomit. The boys ate knockwursts and sauerkraut and Peggy said the odor of the kraut made her nauseous, so she moved to the far side of the table beside Nancy.

Bill moved next to Mike. He was in a conversation with Jimmy about the Abe Reles case.

"Mayor O'Dwyer was as crooked as a cat's back leg," he was saying.

"Och, I don't agree at all," replied Jimmy.

"Then why was he sweating so much when Kefauver was asking him those questions in the Senate?"

"Well, wasn't the same questions being asked of Governor Dewey and no one could say that Dewey was dishonest, although I never voted for him. Wasn't it him that put Lucky Luciano in jail?"

"Look, Jimmy. There was five cops guardin' the sonovabitch Reles and he falls out the hotel window?" asked Bill rhetorically. "There were three detectives on duty there that night: Jimmy Boyle, Victor Robbins, Johnny Moran. And there was two regular foot patrolmen there: a guy by the name of McLaughlin and Frankie Tempone, whose brother I went to high school with."

He paused and drank down his beer before continuing.

"So I'm asking where was the sixth man? You see, there was supposed to be six cops assigned to that shift every night but the night Abe Reles, Kid Blast, goes out the effin' window and does a header onto the boardwalk, there was only five!"

"Well, maybe one of them called in sick that night," said Jimmy.

"Sick? Do you think Forrestal went out the window by himself, too?" asked Bill mockingly.

"Truman's secretary of war you're talking about?" asked Jimmy, confused by Bill's line of reasoning. "The fella that killed himself?"

"Who was the last Irish Catholic you heard threw himself out the window?" replied Bill. "It was Commies like McCarthy says."

"The Commies?" asked Jimmy, surprised.

"Who you gonna believe? A guy named McCarthy or a guy named Hiss or Rosenberg?" said Bill.

"So it's Commies killed Abe Relish too. Is that what you're sayin', Bill? But it was back in '39 it happened."

"But Bill O'Dwyer was Brooklyn DA at the time. Whatever went on, Truman was in on it. Do you think he made O'Dwyer ambassador to Mexico so he could get a suntan?"

Bill poured himself another beer and drank it down.

"Truman got O'Dwyer out of the country because he was the man who knew too much," he continued.

"About what?" asked Jimmy.

"About everything," replied Bill darkly.

He leaned forward and said in a lowered voice, "You know Reles was singin' about Al Anastasia and the rub-out of Moishe Diamond. He was a Teamster official, this Diamond, and probably a Commie."

"Well, I didn't know that at all," said Jimmy.

"There's lots you don't know, being from the other side. Here, there's lots of Commies in the unions."

"They say Mike Quill is a Communist," replied Jimmy. "But he's done a power of good for the Transport Workers."

"But a guy the name of Mike Quill is different from a guy the name of Moishe Diamond."

"Not an Irish Diamond, I take it," said Jimmy with a smile.

"Not an Irish Diamond."

"Now what you're saying is that the Communists killed Abe Relish in revenge for the murder of this Moishe Diamond fella by Albert Anastasia. Is that it?"

"I'm saying where was the sixth cop? Who was he? I'm saying why did O'Dwyer suddenly get sent off to Mexico? I'm asking did Forrestal commit suicide or was he pushed like Kid Blast? I'm asking who promoted Captain Peres to Major? What happened to China? Why did Truman sell out Chiang Kai-shek. I won't be surprised if *he* goes out the window, too!"

"I heard it was because of Sloan Simpson that Truman sent O'Dwyer to Mexico," said Nancy. "So that they could live together without any scandal. It was a love story, Bill dear. It was in Walter Winchell's column."

"What does Winchell know?" asked Bill bitterly. "He's a kike, besides."

Mike saw Annie blink her eyes in pain liked she'd been slapped in the face by the word.

"Why *was* Abe Reles killed, Daddy?" Mike asked as they began the long walk home.

"I heard it was because he turned informer," said Jimmy. "He was go'n to squeal on his pals in Murder Incorporated."

When Mike heard the words "informer" and "squeal" his

heart stopped. Whatever happened with the dynamite, he couldn't squeal. There was no mercy for squealers in this world.

The Dodgers were on the road. As they walked past Ebbets Field, the ball park was empty and silent. Eamonn was walking ahead of him and he reached out and touched the red brick affectionately as if he were patting their dog Sparks's back.

Mike remembered that seventh Series game. The Yankees were ahead 4–2 and the bases were loaded. There were two outs and the count was 3–2 on Jackie Robinson. Kuzava let go the pitch. It was a high curve and Jackie, who was batting over .300 that season, swung. It looked like a homer at first, heading for the fence. But it turned out to be a pop-up. It was hit so hard and high that Furillo and Cox had already crossed the plate with the tying runs and Peewee Reese was racing home from first with the go-ahead and Collins, the Yankee first baseman, lost the ball in the shadow of the stands. The pitcher Kuzava was standing there like an *amadán* with long arms and it looked for sure like the ball was going to drop in for a hit and all the fans in Ebbets were up on their feet and everybody in Brooklyn was up on their feet screaming for the Dodgers to win. And then—and then Billy Martin, the Yankee second baseman, saw it in the corner of his stinking eye and dashed onto the infield grass at the last moment and grabbed the small plummeting sphere of white leather and red stitches just before it hit the ground. The sonuvabitch stole the Series from Brooklyn. The Dodgers shoulda won it 5–4. Five to four and Robinson woulda been a hero. They said that the Dodgers woulda won the Series in '41 if Mickey Owens hadn't dropped that third strike and then thrown the ball away. The history of the Brooklyn Dodgers was like the history of Ireland, full of heroes, heartbreak and tears.

Mike wondered what would have happened if the war hadn't come, if Deucey had gone to Vero Beach for spring training with the Dodgers instead of to Great Lakes for boot camp with the Navy. People said Deucey would have been better than Duke Snider, as good as Snider and Hodges combined. Deucey would have been friends with Jackie Robinson and Newcombe and Campanella and he wouldn't have ever put the dynamite on the roof of the old RKO Grant.

Mike reached over and touched the red bricks of Ebbets Field tenderly, too. The wind gusted and the Texaco sign at the gas station across the avenue where so many home runs had landed over the years began to creak. It sounded like it was crying to Mike, who was full of sorrow for the Dodgers and the great Deuce and the dynamite and himself. It creaked and cried as the wind continued to blow. They walked on and bits of paper and dirt and even dry leaves from the previous fall were lifted up and began to swirl in front of them as the wind intensified. Within a matter of minutes, the sky was transformed and Mike looked up to see the blue heaven disappearing behind huge black thunderheads. Lightning flashed above him and the first drops of rain began to fall onto the warm pavement. The sky opened suddenly and the water came plumping down on them.

The Driscolls and the Doyles took refuge in the entrance way of Hirschhorn's Hosiery with its display cases full of headless mannequins wearing girdles and brassieres. There were legs with garter belts and stockings.

"Instruments of torture," said Jimmy, laughing and looking at the girdles.

Mike couldn't laugh. All he could see were bodies blown apart by dynamite. These plaster casts were signs of things to come when the lightning struck. He looked around at the severed limbs and headless torsos and ran out into the rain again.

"See you home!" he shouted, dashing off.

Charlie made a move to follow him but Nancy held him by the arm.

"Stay where you are. I won't have you spoiling the suit I just got pressed!"

Mike ran through the rain with his head looking up at the sky fearfully. Every time lightning flashed he could feel his heart jump in his chest.

"O Mary Mother! Don't let it hit the RKO! I'll offer up my life to God! O Holy Brighid, protect us from lightning and fire!"

He charged through puddled sidewalks and leaped over rushing rivers of rain in the gutters. He didn't know what he was actually going to do when he got there. He asked himself why he was running toward the danger when everyone he loved was safely behind amid Hirschhorn's girdles and brassieres. What would he do? Rush up and carry the deadly boxes down from the roof? He wanted to stop running and stay safely where he was but he couldn't; his legs carried him forward toward destruction.

It was storming so wildly that the awning couldn't keep his papers dry, so Benny was out spreading a canvas tarp over them. Mike rushed by him. Into the back of the store he went where two wooden phone booths were built into the wall.

Mike closed the folding door behind him and dialed the operator and asked for the police.

"There's dynamite on the roof of the old RKO Grant, four cases of it."

He spoke the words flatly and as he was saying them he was also hearing himself say them. He was listening to the voice as if it belonged to someone else. The voice of an informer. His own voice.

"It'll blow if you don't get it down off there. The Old RKO Grant."

He hung up the phone without giving his name. The dime dropped with such finality into the coin box that he knew his life as it had been was over. The dime was the period at the end of the chapter. Everything from here on out would be something else. Different. Uncertain. Unsure.

Within minutes the square and streets around it were filled with fire trucks and police cars. Sirens, squeezed into the narrow streets, seemed to explode when they reached the open square. Flashing red roof lights turned the rain bloody. Lightning flashed. The fireman and police evacuated the RKO. Hundreds of black people were pushed out into the streets by firemen wearing high rubber hats and high boots and carrying long hatchets. The blacks stood in the pelting rain, their Sunday clothes getting soaked. Water ran off ladies' straw sun hats. Some children were crying while others seemed delighted as they watched the firemen rushing up the metal fire escapes. The police kept pushing the black people across the street behind the statue of Grant who stood guard, as always, eyes south. It was like the Civil War had never ended, Mike thought, imagining Grant coming to life on his noble steed of bronze. A lightning bolt flashed over the square. There was a horrendous clap of thunder and Mike cringed, closing his eyes, expecting the entire building to go up and himself and Grant and everyone else with it. He was terrified but he couldn't run from the danger. He felt he had to stay with these people until the danger was past.

"It hit the armory," said Benny, who had left his store. He was wearing his dirty change apron and chewing on a cigar stub. "The flagpole."

Mike looked down at the armory. The flagpole was directly above the spot where Deucey had hit the home run the year before. If only Deucey had become a Dodger instead of a sailor, he thought. If only he could remake the past, refashion the world according to his own wishes.

"The fireman say it's a bomb," said Benny. "Can you imagine? A bomb. What's this country comin' to?"

Mike had no answer.

"Is that what it is?" he asked, pretending ignorance.

"That's what they say," said Benny, chomping on his cigar. "This I'd expect only from Nazis."

He shook his head and jiggled the silver in his soiled apron like he was making change.

Just then the firemen appeared at the mouth of the alley carrying the dynamite. Four of them, carrying a box each in front, like delivery boys carrying a grocery order. A sigh rose from the crowd that could be heard through the pounding rain.

They put the dynamite on the back of the truck and within moments there was a long cortège of police cars in front and behind the firetruck that moved off and disappeared down the avenue, sirens squealing.

"They take it out to Jamaica Bay and blow it up," said Benny. "It's all over."

"So what was your big hurry before, kid?" he asked, turning to Mike.

Mike was struck dumb. He was convinced for the moment that Benny knew and was going to tell the world.

"Not talkin'?" said Benny smiling. "Got yourself a girl, huh? That's the only reason a guy runs around in a thunderstorm. Girls. I wish I was your age, kid. Startin' out again. Enjoy it."

Mike smiled inanely, still terrified that Benny would guess the real reason.

"Women!" said Benny and returned to his store taking the canvas off his papers as he walked in.

IT HAD STOPPED raining. The storm had passed as quickly as it had come. The fire trucks vanished too, and the police cars, except for one that sat parked in front of the marquee, which no longer advertised a double feature but CHRIST CRUCIFIED alone in big black letters.

Traffic began to move through the streets again. Sunday drivers, strange faces peering through the windshields wondering what had caused the delay. Sunlight danced through the raindrops that clung to the fire escapes and fences, changing the tenements into old holy books covered with precious stones.

The air smelled sweet and hummed with human voices. The colored people were still standing around the statue of Grant, some of the women were crying, now that the danger was passed.

Mike approached a black boy about his own age who was standing looking up at the roof of the RKO. There was a cop up there looking out across the neighborhood.

"Did anyone get hurt?" Mike asked.

"Whatchou care, white boy?" replied the boy, spitting the words out of his mouth.

This was the last thing that Mike had expected to hear. For a moment he had forgotten the way it was.

"Fuck you, too," he said, his voice turning cold. He turned on his heel and walked toward his house.

"Fuckin' nigguhs," he said to himself as he walked. "No wonder people hate 'em. Bunch of assholes."

MIKE WAS SITTING on the stoop in front of his house when he saw his pal Charlie trotting towards him. He didn't want to face Charlie, for he knew that Charlie would put two and two together. But there was no escape.

"Hear what happened?" asked Charlie.

"Yeah," answered Mike.

"It was you, wasn't it?" asked Charlie. "Called the cops. Sissy. Squealer."

"I ain't no squealer or no sissy. I didn't call no cops."

"Oh yeah, well, why did you run and leave us back in Hirschhorn's then?"

"I had to call a girl," said Mike, making use of Benny's idea.

"A girl? What girl?"

"I ain't sayin'," said Mike.

"You're bullshittin'. You called the cops, you fink."

"I tell you I called a girl. I was supposed to go to the movies with her today. Meet her there."

"Well, who is she? I ain't gonna believe you unless you tell me her name."

"Okay. It was your cousin Tiny."

"Oh yeah? You and Tiny," Charlie giggled. "Well, I'm gonna talk to her and if she don't back you up I'm gonna talk to my Uncle Deucey."

"Some pal you are," said Mike.

Charlie started to run off.

"Where you goin'?" Mike shouted after him.

"To talk to Tiny."

He sped off.

Mike knew it would be useless to follow him. His family didn't have a phone and he didn't have another dime to call Tiny. All he could do was hope that Tiny would back up his story. She'd always been nice to him in the past. His heart sank in his chest as he resigned himself to fate.

A few minutes later, the great Deucey appeared at the corner. He was with Bunny Imp. Mike tried to make himself smaller by crowding in next to the baluster of the stoop. The two men were looking up at the roof of the RKO. The cop was still up there on guard. He had his hat off and Mike saw it was O'Ruarke of the Flaming Head who'd cuffed him for shooting carpets. The Imp was talking, his hands cutting through the air, and Deucey was shaking his head. Then he patted Deucey on the shoulder as if to calm him down. Mike was way too far away to hear anything. The two men disappeared into Santo's Bakery.

That night there was nothing but talk about the dynamite and bombs at the Driscolls'. Annie made the tea and they had pot roast sandwiches and lettuce and tomato and then toast and jelly. Mike told his family the same lie he'd told his pal except he didn't mention Tiny's name and they didn't ask for it.

"Our Michael's growing up," said Annie.

"He's got no personality," said Peggy. "No girl in her right mind would go to the movies with a creep like him."

Eamonn smirked.

His father told the tale about the Volunteers trying to blow up the police barracks in his home area during the Troubles. The walls were three foot thick of stone and the windows covered with iron plate and the boyos couldn't blow it open no matter how hard they tried, according to his father. It was only when one of the Peelers who was sympathetic to the Cause gave them the password that they were able to get in.

"Och, I'll tell ye those *seoiníní* was surprised looking up from their cards and seeing them Republican gun barrels staring at them. They was playin' twenty-fives, they was. Well, the Volunteers took them prisoner and they blew the place up with a fine bomb they'd made for the occasion. They destroyed all the records too. It was great day for ould Éire it was that! That's what bombs is for. Blowing up police barracks and army camps.

Not for blowing up churches! Sure it's a coward who'd think of doing such a thing!"

Of course Mike knew that the great Deucey Doyle was no coward but it did his heart good to hear his father say that. But he couldn't share any of his emotional turmoil with his family because he didn't want anyone to know he'd squealed no matter what—even if he was right.

Jimmy continued talking about the Troubles and about the bad times in the three centuries prior to them. He got so full of emotion about the whole thing that Mike knew he'd have to sing and he stood up at the kitchen table behind the teapot and the ruins of supper and sang *"Róisín Dubh,"* about how it was a long journey he'd made from yesterday to today and how he'd walked the length of Erin searching for that fragrant branch of womanhood. He sang that the sea would turn to red waves and the sky to blood and that the gore of battle would be on the backs of the hills and that every mountain and every bog throughout the land would quake that day before death would come to take that dark rose that was Ireland.

For Mike it was like hearing the song for the first time. Tears came to his eyes. Raw tears lacking sentiment.

Mike was waiting for the knock on the door all evening and when it came he wasn't surprised. Peggy went to the door thinking it was one of her friends. But he knew it was Charlie come to pronounce the death sentence or whatever they did to guys who turned out to be squealers.

Peggy came back disappointed.

"It's that creep Charlie, for you," she said to Mike.

Mike walked slowly to the door.

"Everything's okay," said his friend. "I talked to Tiny and she backed up what you said."

Mike was so relieved he felt like kissing his friend. But he had to pretend he was angry that his honor had been questioned.

"Well, next time you'll know better than to go accusin' people," he said gruffly.

He slammed the door as part of the act. As soon as the door was shut he leaned up against it and sighed, letting himself slide to the floor like a empty sack.

The next day after school, Mike went over to Tiny's house to thank her for lying. She looked surprised.

"I didn't lie," she said.

"No?" Mike asked shocked. "Didn't Charlie ask you if I'd called you?"

"Yes. I said you hadn't. And then he asked something about us going to the movies together. It was all very confusing. I hope I didn't say the wrong thing."

"No, that's okay. How were you supposed to know?"

"Know what?"

"Naw, don't worry. It's nothing important."

"It must be or you wouldn't have come all the way over here to thank me for something I didn't do. C'mon," she said, "tell me. Didn't I trust you enough to tell you my dream about the Smiling Clown?"

Maybe he should tell her. Maybe he'd feel a little easier if he shared the burden with someone. But how could he trust her? This wasn't dream stuff, this was the real thing.

"I'd like to tell, but I can't. If I was gonna tell anyone, I would tell you." He looked down at his feet as he spoke.

"That's okay," she said, disappointed. "But maybe we could go to the movies together? After all, you told Charlie that we were going."

"Maybe," he said. "Maybe I can meet you next Sunday at the Loewies. There's a good show."

"Next Sunday at the Loew's," she said, correcting his pronunciation. "That sounds fine."

"By the candy counter at one o'clock."

Even if he hadn't told her the story, Mike felt relieved that she knew there was a story. He no longer felt quite so lonely. Mike was confused about Charlie. It took him a while until he figured it out. Charlie was covering up for him. It was that simple. What a pal! What a friend! What had he ever done for Charlie that could match this?

That night Deucey Doyle beat Tommy the Hat in the Bedford Rest beergarden. He beat him with a baseball bat and Tommy ran out on the street where he collapsed unconscious. The ambulance came and took him to the Swedish Hospital where he remained in a coma.

The cops arrested Deucey on the spot. He didn't try to escape. He was at the bar drinking when the cops took him.

Nobody knew why Deucey beat Tommy the Hat. There'd been no angry words between them according to the bartender. He said that Deucey had been drinking boilermakers by himself when The Hat came in. They nodded to each other, The Hat and Deucey. But they didn't talk. About ten minutes later, Deucey went into the backroom of the bar where the Brevoort Boys kept their stickball supplies and T-shirts. He came out with the baseball bat in his hand, and when he was passing by

The Hat he just stopped and walloped him with it. He didn't say anything. Not a word. He kept hitting him until the bartender and the other customers got the bat away from him. By that time Tommy the Hat had escaped out onto the sidewalk where he keeled over into the gutter.

When the Deuce calmed down he went back to his drink. He had two more quick ones before the cops put the cuffs on him.

That was the story Mickey Reilly, the bartender, told and that was the story that got repeated throughout Precious Blood for the next week while Tommy the Hat lay unconscious in the hospital. Nobody knew why Deucey had done what he'd done except Mike and Charlie and Bunny Imp. Deucey thought that Tommy the Hat had squealed to the cops about the dynamite. So Deucey was teaching him a lesson. The cops picked up Bunny for questioning but let him go after a couple of hours.

Charlie hadn't spoken to Mike since Sunday night when he had lied and told him his story checked out. If he was covering for Mike, he wasn't forgiving him for being a fink. Mike had hoped that Charlie would soon forgive him and they could get on with the business of being best pals, which they had been since before kindergarten. Now with Tommy the Hat in a coma and Deucey in jail, there was no chance of that. It was his fault that Tommy was near death. He was the guilty one. He was the one who should have been in the hospital. It was all his fault. Deucey had only done what they did to finks and squealers.

Every day Mike made a "visit" to church after school to pray for Tommy the Hat's recovery. He would kneel in the aisle below the stained glass window and let the colored light rain down on his bare head and his folded hands. It was the Lazarus

window showing *Christ Raising Lazarus from the Tomb* just as
He would raise Himself from the tomb soon after.

Mike prayed that Christ would raise Tommy the Hat out of
his coma. "Take up your bed, Tommy, and walk."

THE LAZARUS MIRACLE wasn't the only miracle happening in
a window. Tiny was the first to see it and afterwards she called it
"her" miracle even though Eamonn said it was really Terry
Doyle's miracle because he was the "proximate cause" of it—
since Eamonn had entered high school he'd grown bigger and
so had his words. Everybody else called it the miracle in Catalano's window because that's what it was.

Tiny was on her way to bring her mother a snack. Eileen was
working that afternoon in Womrath's bookstore. Well, Tiny
was passing in front of Kleinberg's Laundry and she looked
over to see the time. It was 3:14 on the clock in the laundry
window. (Mike would later remember that 3:14 P.M. was the
same hour and minute that the great Deucey had hit the long
historic ball—only the days were different. It was Friday instead of Sunday.) Her eyes moved over to the window of Catalano's grocery store, which came right after Kleinberg's, and
she saw the face in the glass. It was the holy face, the face of she
who had suffered long. Tiny recognized her immediately.
Didn't she have a statue of her at home with a screw-off bottom
where she kept rosary beads and medals?

It was the Blessed Mother, without doubt, there in the glass.

Tiny fell to her knees and soon the whole street was filled with the word "miracle."

"Miracle!"

"It's a miracle!"

"Our Lady's in the window!"

"My God, I can see her face!"

Soon the sidewalk in front of Catalano's store was crowded with kneeling children and a couple of old ladies with canes and thick stockings who seemed from the joyous look on their faces to have been waiting for something marvelous like this their entire lives.

MIKE CROUCHED DOWN next to Vinnie Collucci and asked him what was going on.

"It's Our Lady. She's appeared in the window," said Vinnie of the Long Toes.

Maybe this was a sign that Tommy the Hat would get well, Mike thought, that things would turn to the good again, that life would be what it was before the dynamite had destroyed it, destroyed it without ever blowing up. Mike searched the window with eyes hungry for peace and solace. He couldn't see anything. The window looked normal to him. Fancy pears, apples, oranges wrapped in tissue paper. Broccoli, heads of cauliflower neatly trimmed without bruise or blemish. The Burkes used to get their vegetables at Catalano's when his mother had worked for them. She said the Catalanos had had a good bit of the "carriage trade" in the old days when there was a "carriage trade" in Brooklyn and you could still see it in the quality and in the care they gave their fruit and vegetables.

Out of this vegetable landscape rose a pyramid of Italian olive oil in silver tins, a green ziggurat of Heinz Vegetarian Baked Beans, a Mayan temple built of corned beef from the Argentine in red trapezoidal cans with metal keys. Glass towers of Irish thick-cut marmalade and Lyle's Golden Syrup from Liverpool rounded out the skyline in gold and green enamel. Behind all this were the beaming faces of the Miss Rheingold Beer contestants rising like sanitized fertility goddesses on immense red-framed billboards.

"I can't see her," said Mike, disturbed.

He was afraid that he was unworthy to see her, that everything that Brother Barometer had ever said about his sinfully proud personality was in fact true, and that the Blessed Mother was therefore denying him the ability to see her, as punishment.

"All I can see is food," he said.

"She's not inside the window," said Vinnie. "She's in the glass. Up in the corner."

He pointed with his index finger. The index finger was the same as the second toe, Mike found himself thinking as he searched the glass at which it pointed.

There she was, in the corner! He felt relieved and elated. The face was shadowy and she was wearing a robe and he could see the folding contours in the glass.

"It's from the bottles," explained Vinnie. "A box of empties on the floor. You see, Terry Doyle delivered an order to Mrs.

Carney over on St. Mark's Avenue and she gave him his tip in empty beer bottles. Terry took the bottles back to the store and as soon as he put the box down the Blessed Virgin appeared in the glass of the window. Isn't that something?"

"Amazing," said Mike.

"Tiny saw the apparition first," said Vinnie. "She's kneeling up by the crate of lettuce."

The Catalanos kept the cheaper vegetables out front on the sidewalk. Mike looked up and saw the crown of her dark head. He elbowed and shouldered his way through the wedge of worshippers until he was next to Tiny.

"A real miracle," he whispered.

"And I saw it first," she whispered back. "I can scarcely believe it. Isn't she beautiful?"

"Yeah, just like the pictures of her. The statues," said Mike. "Maybe this means that Tommy the Hat will get all right again and they'll let Deucey go out of jail."

"I've already asked for the very same thing. My mother is very upset about Uncle Deucey. That's why I was bringing her this snack. She hasn't eaten a thing since it happened. She looks like a ghost."

"I thought they didn't talk, her and Deucey?"

"They don't since the war. But she loves him. I think she loves him as much as she does me."

"Then why don't they be friends?"

"Something happened between them after Grandma died. It's a secret and she won't tell me. My parents argue about it though. Often when they're angry with each other, I hear Uncle Deucey's name come up."

"Parents all argue," he replied. "That's the way grownups are. Always arguing about something. Complaining."

"I think Mary can straighten it out. After all, she was a mother," Tiny said, closing her eyes.

She was quiet for a minute as if deep in prayer.

"How's *your* secret?" she asked.

"That's why I'm hopin' The Hat recovers," said Mike.

"Your secret has a connection with Tommy the Hat and my uncle Deucey?"

"Yeah," he mumbled.

"Then why don't you tell me?"

How could he tell this girl that he was a squealer, a fink and informer? What would she think when she found out it was his fault that her uncle was in jail? He thought of Judas who had betrayed Christ.

"I'll tell you about about it when everything's okay again. I promise."

Mike heard Vinnie Collucci's voice behind them. He was reciting the Litany of the Blessed Virgin. For the first time the voice of this rival sounded pleasant and even sonorous to Mike, so deeply did he want a miracle. Mary was God's mother and she was the mother of mankind. If God wouldn't listen to your prayer, she would. She was sympathetic. And God would listen to her because she was His mother.

> ". . . Virgin most powerful,
> "Virgin most merciful,
> "Virgin most faithful,

"Mirror of justice,
"Seat of wisdom,
"Cause of our joy,
"Spiritual vessel,
"Vessel of honor,
"Singular vessel of devotion,
"Mystical rose,
"Tower of David,
"Tower of ivory,
"House of gold,
"Ark of the covenant,
"Gate of heaven,
"Morning star,
"Health of the sick,
"Refuge of sinners,
"Comforter of the afflicted . . ."

When the Litany was ended, Vinnie began on the rosary and the crowd of children and some more old ladies did the responses. Mrs. Catalano came out of the store with Terry Doyle. Terry was beaming, satisfaction shooting from each pore in his skin. He couldn't help but flex his uncovered muscles. He was wearing a T-shirt with the sleeves rolled up around his shoulders.

The sidewalk was jammed with children and the pedestrians had to go out into the street to get past. Cars and trucks had to stop to let them by. Horns honked and many foul words flew over the bowed heads of the worshippers.

"Children," Mrs. Catalano said in a pause between the decades of the rosary, "please get up. You'll get all dirty kneeling on the sidewalk. What will your mothers say?"

"We're doing it for Her," said Vinnie, nodding to the window.

"Terry," she said in a low voice, "look what you've done to me. These kids! All these people and nobody buying anything!"

She looked up at heaven imploringly.

A police car pulled up in front of the store.

"Officer O'Ruarke," said Mrs. Catalano, "thank God you're here."

He made his way through the kneeling crowd. She explained the situation to him. He inspected the window.

"This miracle will put me out of business," she said. "The Depression didn't do it but this will. I can't have these children kneeling in front of my store. It'll scare away the customers. Who's gonna buy a pound of pears when you have the Madonna in the window?"

"Why don't you move the box?" he asked.

"Eh, Officer, I'm a Catholic. I don't want to destroy a miracle. I just don't want anyone to get hurt."

"I can understand," said O'Ruarke, shaking his fiery head sympathetically.

Eamonn came along from the subway, his heavy high school textbooks under his arm. Mike and Tiny showed him the Virgin's face. He knelt down and blessed himself solemnly, losing himself in silent prayer. Mike wondered if he himself ever looked that holy when he was praying.

O'Ruarke turned to the children. Mike cringed a little. Every time he saw O'Ruarke something jumped inside him.

"Okay, kids, ladies! Break it up. Move along. You're obstructing a public way here, which is a violation of the New York City Code. Get up off your knees and let the pedestrians pass. Move it along, kids. We don't want anyone getting hurt!"

Nobody moved.

"If you don't clear the way, I may be forced to arrest youse!" he said solemnly in measured tones.

"I'm willing to suffer imprisonment for the Faith!" said Eamonn. "Martyrdom even."

"Yes, throw us to the lions, Officer," said Vinnie.

O'Ruarke of the Fiery Head blew hot breath through his lips like a dragon trying to keep its temper.

"I'll go to Precious Blood and get a priest," he said, turning to Mrs. Catalano.

"I'll go with you, Officer," announced Eamonn, leaving his books next to Mike. "I was an altar boy and know all the priests."

"Me, too," said Vinnie, getting up.

"One is enough for the job," said the cop, waving him off.

Vinnie didn't listen to him. He piled into the dark green and white Ford, next to Eamonn. Mike felt kind of jealous of Eamonn and Vinnie, getting a lift in a cop car. He figured that the only ride O'Ruarke would ever give him would be to the Raymond Street Jail, with his hands cuffed behind him. The kind of ride they'd given Deucey Sunday night.

Five minutes later, the car was back and Monsignor Shugrue stepped out of its front passenger-side door. He was wearing his biretta with the purple pom-pom and his purple satin belly band. His cape fluttered behind him, cloaking children and old ladies, as he made his way through the crowd. He talked to Mrs. Catalano and to Terry Doyle. Tiny went up to him and pointed out the Virgin's face.

"I saw her first," she said proudly.

Shugrue took off his biretta and placed it on the stand, where it rested on a large head of cabbage. He stood squarely in front of the window and looked up at the apparition.

Vinnie began the rosary again, speeding from "Hail Mary" to ". . . thy womb, Jesus" while the others rushed in reply from "Holy Mary" to ". . . the hour of our death. Amen." These were experts at prayer, school children and old ladies. If their repetition was swift, mechanical and impersonal, this very impersonality lent it a truly otherworldly quality.

After about two minutes of staring, the monsignor bowed his head and opened his palms in a liturgical gesture. His mouth moved as he recited some Latin prayers. Eamonn stood attentive, at a respectful distance from the pastor, like an off-duty altar boy, still religious-looking in his civilian clothes.

"Officer O'Ruarke, please move the box," Shugrue said. "I've prayed for guidance and this is the answer I've received."

O'Ruarke walked slowly into the doorway, past Terry Doyle who was looking disappointed and Mrs. Catalano who was looking apprehensive if hopeful. O'Ruarke touched the cardboard box filled with empty quart beer bottles very gingerly with the tip of his enormous black shining shoe as if he were expecting to get an electric shock. The children and old ladies stopped reciting the rosary. All onlookers were silent. The traffic appeared to have halted and the horns and the impatient shouts stopped for the moment. Mike took Tiny by the hand and they both held their breath together. The fiery-headed policeman pushed gently. The tinkling of the empty bottles could be heard echoing in the silent street. The Virgin vanished. Her beatific face and her long shadowy robes were no more. Only the beaming smiles of the Rheingold beer girls looking silly and sacrilegious remained in the window.

Mike and Tiny sighed with disappointment.

"You can't get no miracle outta no beer bottles," said a familiar voice.

Mike looked behind. It was his pal Charlie. He smiled at him.

"Just as I thought, Officer," announced the pastor in triumph.

For there was nothing in the world that the Catholic clergy liked to do more than debunk local miracles. It seemed to manifest to them and to perhaps some curious potential Catholics, they hoped, the basic rationality of their faith.

Mike and Tiny however were shocked by the pastor's attitude.

"Now, move the bottles back to their original position," said Shugrue.

O'Ruarke stepped to the far side of the box and nudged it again with his great black shoe—less fearful this time. The face of the Blessed Mother did not reappear.

"A mere *fata morgana*, my children," announced Shugrue,

turning toward the kneeling would-be worshippers. "A mere mirage such as appears in the great Sahara. A quirk of light. No miracle. No miracle."

Mike had let Tiny's hand go as soon as he saw Charlie was behind him. Now she began to cry and he had to take her hand again and rub it just as he remembered his mother rubbing his when he was little and afraid. He looked sheepishly behind but Charlie was no longer there. He was relieved and disappointed at the same time. For he thought that his pal might be coming round, having knelt behind them and spoken—even if his words were cynical.

"I guess Charlie was right," said Tiny between sniffles. "One can't expect miracles to come from beer bottles."

"Go home, children. We appreciate your devotion," announced the monsignor, recovering his biretta from the cabbage.

"You heard the monsignor," said O'Ruarke. "Break it up and move along. It's all over."

"Is there any word on Tommy the Hat, Officer O'Ruarke?" asked Mrs. Catalano. "You know he used to deliver for me when he was a teenager."

"I'm sorry. He expired a couple of hours ago without recovering consciousness," O'Ruarke replied sympathetically in the bureaucratic way of cops.

"*Madonna, riposi in pace!* Tommy! *Il mio povero ragazzo!*"

Tears ran from her eyes and she retreated into the store out of the gaze of customers.

"That means that that Doyle fellow will be held for murder, doesn't it?" said Shugrue.

"Right. He's in big trouble, Monsignor. Big trouble," said O'Ruarke, his voice growing hard again as he spoke.

The cop and the pastor walked off, Eamonn and Vinnie at their heels.

Tiny burst into more tears now and her whole body was shaking and Mike put his arm around her shoulder and she leaned over and rested her body against his and he could feel her soft little breasts pressing against his shirt and tie for he was still wearing his school clothes. Those soft little breasts made him feel so good at the same time that he was feeling terrible because of Tommy's death and because he was the cause of it and because the great Deucey would die in the electric chair in Sing Sing and he would be the cause of that, too. It wasn't Deucey who was the murderer, it was himself.

Like the God whom he could never understand and half-hated, he had allowed evil to come into the world. If he hadn't squealed, the storm would have passed and the dynamite would not have blown because, as Benny had pointed out, the lightning struck the armory and lightning always strikes the highest point. Therefore if he had remembered that, if he had used his brains and not been such a sissy, he would have stayed cool like his pal Charlie, who had that heroic calm that went back to Fionn and the Fianna. And the dynamite wouldn't have exploded and Bunny Imp would have persuaded Deucey to let Tommy the Hat sell all four boxes of it and they would have gone to the racetrack with the money and the coloreds would have been safe and that kid wouldn't have called him a "white boy" and everything would have been like it was and his pal Charlie would still have been his pal and he wouldn't have ever been a squealer, a fink, an informer, like Arnold Schuster or Kid Blast.

How could he tell Tiny it was him, that he was responsible for the whole awful situation? How could her little breasts feel so wonderfully soft, in a world without miracles? He began to cry himself and she hugged him closer to her.

THE STORY WAS going round Precious Blood that weekend but Mike didn't hear it until Monday at the noon recess in the schoolyard. Charlie had avoided his eyes all morning in the classroom. Mike was standing alone in the yard with his back against the American handball court.

"Bastard! Bastard!" they were yelling. "Deucey is a bastard! Bastard! Bastard!"

Boys from his class had Charlie surrounded and he was swinging at them like mad as they taunted him. His face was twisted with hate, one eye like a burning coal and the other bulging out of its socket as if it would explode, his hair standing on end and his skin glowing like a small sun as he whirled about smashing noses.

Mike ran across the yard and jumped into the battle, punching. All the rage that was pent up within him came out and he even kicked boys who were down, something which he hadn't done before. It wasn't long before the taunters retreated before the furious fists of Mike and Charlie.

"Whatta they mean calling Deucey a bastard?" asked Mike,

working his fists, his body trembling with adrenaline after the battle.

"Why don't you ask your father?" said Charlie, sarcastically.

"My father? What's my father have to do with it?"

"He's my Uncle Deucey's real father. Haven't you heard? And my Aunt Eileen, she's his mother and not his sister like I always thought!"

Mike felt his knees giving way and he knew he'd fall if he didn't run, so he ran.

He ran through the milling students and out the front gate and kept running. He ran for blocks. The more he ran the less he felt he could stop and he found himself on the trail to the park, the route he and his friends followed on the way to play baseball and he ran past the Brooklyn Museum with its column and dome and statues of the great men of history, heroes three times the size of life, and he didn't look up at them and read their names like he always did but kept his eyes on the ground in front of him. He ran into the Botanical Gardens, past the flowers and bushes with their names on small glazed metal signs, and he didn't stop to read one of them or to try to commit its Latin to memory. He ran till he collapsed in the Cherry Blossom Esplanade and there was no one there at all, no Japanese, no Americans, and all the blossoms had fallen from the trees and the whole world seemed naked.

It all made sense now, why Deucey had gotten so mad when the colored minister called him a "bastard" and how angrily he'd reacted to Tommy the Hat mocking him in the Joy that morning. It all made sense. The mystery of Deucey Doyle was solved.

Mike didn't go back to school that afternoon. He stayed out until sundown, fearful of being seen and mocked in the streets.

When he got home his mother didn't even say hello to him. She was sitting in a chair staring out the window. Eamonn was reading a missal in the bedroom and Peggy's eyes were red from crying. Michael didn't know what to say to his father.

He could hear his parents arguing in the living room late that night. His father kept repeating that it was "an accident of fate."

"Things like this just happen, *mo mhuirnín*," he said over and over to Annie. "Just happen.

"I don't feel like Deucey's father at all!

"Eileen Evans! It was so long ago that I forgot about it entirely!"

Such was what Mike heard his father say through the crack in the door.

His father was gone when he woke up the next morning and he never returned.

"I can't live with your father after what he did to us," was all Annie would say about it.

She couldn't explain to them outright that she suspected that Jimmy had been going to bed with Eileen Evans all those years and that she had been made a fool of, all those nights he was supposed to be working late and Mr. Evans off working on Broadway. She kept remembering the big moons of eyes Jimmy had when they used play canasta. No wonder! What a fool she'd been! A laughing stock! And they'd get word of it at home and it would spread all over the glen and when she thought of all the letters she'd written praising her Jimmy and his fine sweet words and gift of song and such a hard worker too! She couldn't share her suspicions because they made her feel so loathsome. But the children got the message of the vacant stare out the window.

Eamonn went off to a seminary in upstate New York to study for the priesthood, to be closer to God and farther from the source of embarrassment.

Peggy started to really believe that she was from another planet and she stayed out late at night and dated boys all the time to prove her independence.

Mike had no escape. He was the cause of the all the misfortune and how could he escape from himself?

Annie got a job as an nurse's aide in the hospital. It didn't pay decently and Jimmy would send her money through Bill Doyle.

Bill got him that job in the Navy Yard he'd always been offering him. Jimmy needed the extra money since he had to get an apartment for himself in addition to supporting Annie and the kids. Ironically, it was Deucey's old ship, the aircraft carrier *Franklin*, they were working together on. The hero ship. The ship the Japs couldn't sink.

Of course, Bill had always guessed the true story of Deucey's origins. Eileen had kept it a secret all those years from everyone but her husband, and she had told her brother the facts only on the day they'd got the news that Deucey would be charged with murder. But, as a boy, Bill had seen Eileen and Jimmy Driscoll coming down from the roof that night, after he he'd succeeded in escaping from the Old Man's blows. And he knew from the look of them what had gone on between them. So he wasn't shocked by her revelation.

Even though as an adult he was full of hate, he never developed a grudge against Jimmy Driscoll and always kept a soft spot for him in his heart. Perhaps this was because it all happened so long ago, at a time before his heart had become totally closed to new experience. Perhaps, too, it was revenge on the Old Man. He couldn't help feeling satisfaction and a kind of joy, even, remembering the old tyrant's humiliation at Eileen's getting pregnant. Perhaps it was also because he had looked up to Jimmy Driscoll when he was young and he'd wanted to be like him because you could actually talk to him and he was so unlike the Old Man. Even now when he often considered Jimmy a fool, a romantic, a simple-minded bog-trotter, a dupe of the Commies, there was a part of Bill that still wanted to be like him. There was something clean about him he admired and didn't feel in himself.

Nobody knew who'd spread the story about Jimmy being the Deucey's father but Annie couldn't help suspecting Nancy. She figured it was Nancy's revenge on the Shiels for having grass for seven cows while the Mac Orraistíns hadn't enough for one and were forced to keep goats and send their sons off to Alba for the *préataí* harvest.

She also thought that Jimmy's working on the ship was a kind of retribution. She had thrown him out even though she still loved him and now he was paying her back by trampling on her innermost fears, making mockery of them. She accepted his money because she had no other choice in the matter. . . .

.   .   .

IT WAS MORNING, that winter, and Bill couldn't stand the
sound of the hammers below decks. He was hung over and he
told Jimmy and the rest of his gang that he had business with
the section chief, topside. He found himself a cubbyhole in the
carrier's island and took a few slugs out of the half-pint he had
as a hair of the dog. He lay down and covered himself with a
tarpaulin so he could sleep without being seen. A nap would do
the trick for the headache. He was in a half-dreaming, half-
waking state and a little voice was telling him that he would
stick with the beer that night. A couple of beers at lunch and a
couple more on Flushing Avenue before he got the bus for
home. He could smell the metal stink of the welding torches
and he wondered how anybody could do welding with a
hangover.

He was drifting off when his throat began to tickle. He
cleared it several times. He thought he might be getting a cold.
His phlegm tasted bitter. He stopped drifting. He couldn't
breathe. He was drowning. He was choking. He threw off the
tarp and jumped up. Smoke was coming into the hatch. Black
acrid smoke. He heard voices screaming.

He was going to get to safety when he suddenly remembered
that his gang was below decks and that Jimmy Driscoll was
down there too.

"Fuckin' bullshit!" he muttered. "Probably some fuckin'
nigger not payin' attention to what he was doin'!"

A fire-fighting squad was collecting on the main aircraft
elevator on the flight deck. He joined them, and as the huge
metal square sank from sight into the billowing smoke that rose

from the guts of the ship they looked like a group of souls descending into Hell. This was the last that was seen of Bill Doyle alive.

ANNIE WAS ON the eighth floor of the hospital that morning. When she saw the black cloud rising from the Navy Yard she knew immediately what it meant. When she heard the knock on the apartment door that evening, she hoped it would be Jimmy standing there but she knew it wasn't. And when the naval officer came in, his chest bedecked with ribbons, and said she could be proud that Jimmy had "died for his country," she knew that that wasn't true. He died because he'd been born at the Hour of the Handsome Man and all her swimming had been in vain.

MIKE EXPECTED THE world to stop when his father died. But it didn't. Not for a second. The streets were busy. The Catalanos unloaded vegetables. Women shopped. Money changed hands. The chimes of cash registers mingled with the bells of Precious Blood on the quarter hour. Working men still waited for trolleys, cigarettes smoking in their mouths. They squinted. They laughed. They talked. They read newspapers unfolded from back pockets. Short leather jackets. Heavy shoes. Protective boots.

For a while he couldn't accept it and he kept expecting to see

Jimmy coming round the corner in the evening to say it all had been a huge practical joke he'd thought up. But he never came.

Mike took to walking the dog like his father had done and kept hoping to see him again in the crowd outside of Benny's. He would have settled for a shadowy presence like the Virgin in the window. But there was nothing of the kind. Nobody came back from the dead ever. Nobody ever except Jesus Christ, they said. But no one had seen Him lately either.

There was no escape from death. There was no escape from life. Life went on. It had room for a hundred rising suns in a hundred tenement windows but none for one dead man to eat a soft-boiled egg in. The harsh horns of trucks squeezed every last inch out of the street. Each day the mornings moved ahead.

IT WAS THE coloreds' fault. The niggers. The coons. It was like Bill Doyle always said: They were destroying Brooklyn. If it hadn't been for the coons moving into the RKO, Deucey would have never put the dynamite on the roof. If it hadn't been for that coon minister calling Deucey a "bastard," Tommy the Hat would have still been alive and the great Deucey wouldn't have been serving a twenty-year term in Sing Sing. Bill Doyle would have been alive too. And most of all, his own father would never have died and he wouldn't have had to feel like he'd killed him with his squealing to the cops. Yes, his father would still be dancing every St. Patrick's day over the smooth floors of Precious Blood auditorium, over the noble wood, unblemished like the bodies of the ancient *taoisigh*. And Charlie would still have been his friend and he wouldn't be lonely like he was and he wouldn't have to hide every time he saw Tiny coming down the block, the love of his life he couldn't look in the eye. Indeed, it was that nigger minister's fault. He was the one who moved his church into the Grant, he was the one who'd called Deucey that name, "bastard." He was the one who really should be dead.

Mike went down into the cellar and walked to the lumber room. He pulled the dresser out from the wall, the dresser his father would never get the opportunity to repair and refinish. The painting of the Smiling Clown fell over on the floor. He paid no attention to it. He removed the loose brick and took out Deucey's gun, unwrapping it from the oily rag. He hid the gun under his jacket.

He went to the square and stood in the shadow under the darkened marquee, which still preached CHRIST CRU-CIFIED in large letters. It was Monday night, the night the nigger minister always stayed late. Mike had been watching him for weeks. It was chilly and Mike shivered as he waited, his hand touching the cold metal of the revolver. He heard the minister closing the door and he saw him coming through the foyer. He let him come out and turn to lock the door. He waited till the nigger had the key in the lock. He took the pistol out of his jacket and pointed it at him. He aimed at his temple, at the brown curve of his ear. He hesitated for a moment before pressing the trigger. Then, he felt a hand on his arm. A small hand that had no warmth in it at all.

"Ná scaoil, mo chroí istigh. Má scaoileann tú, cha dtig leat teacht

as riamh is choíche. Caith uait an t-arm sin." said a small voice. "Don't shoot, my heart's darling. If you shoot, you'll never get out of it ever. Throw that gun away."

Mike looked into the pale eyes and he knew it was Wee Kitty. He lowered his arm and put the gun back in his jacket. He looked again and it was Tiny he saw this time standing next to him and she was holding his wrist.

"Can I help you young people?" asked the minister, looking over at them curiously.

"No," Mike replied. "We're okay."

"No, Reverend," added Tiny, well-mannered.

The minister drove off in his car and Mike and Tiny walked away down the block without speaking. They walked past her building and the great armory with its frightening fist sticking into the black night. They crossed the street and Mike opened his coat and tossed the revolver down the sewer on the corner, the very same sewer that the great Deucey's home run had disappeared down. They went to Bauer's soda fountain and they bought ice-cream sodas and looked at each other.

On the way home to her house they walked up Brevoort. He took her down his cellar and showed her the painting of the Smiling Clown. She was shocked seeing it. She thought it was still in her parents' closet and was really impressed that Mike had stolen it for her sake and had never even bothered to tell her about it.

"Let's burn it," she said after staring at the dreaded face for a while.

Mike opened the door of the furnace and Tiny threw the

painting in. The smile went up in flames. The smile with the knife in it.

"This will be our secret," she said, watching the fire.

They stood against the wall then and kissed. She let him feel her breasts.

ABOUT THE AUTHOR

Bill O'Sullivan was born in Brooklyn of Irish parents. After graduating from Brooklyn College, he served in the U.S. Army in Vietnam, and later studied in Austria and Mexico. He writes in Irish and English.